Alabaster Stavinof

And The Pink Cartridge For Two

Alabaster Stavinof

And The Pink Cartridge For Two

W. M. SHARP

ACKNOWLEDGEMENTS

Dedicated to:
My
Father & Mother

FOREWORD

It's a highly psychological book, filled with murder, suspense, sex, violence, comedy, pain, laughter, and a sensible array of wholesomeness; splashed with a glass of milk. But fear not if you're lactose intolerant, we will not be getting wet. One man, one duck, one way of looking at many views of the world and reality; step inside this spaceship as we tunnel forty leagues into the ground, and come out the other side unscathed. Yet you will feel like we have not gone anywhere at all; or will you?

In a world of occupied space, one man has the power over his own reality. This man, let's call him "Al", is speaking to you from the pages you're reading right now. The book, on the other hand, is a multi-tiered venture about a guy and his duck roommate, *[A real "party fowl," who works at a Chinese-food restaurant]*, which is one man's understanding of reality from his point of view. Like eating a Turchuck *[A Turkey, Chicken, and Duck; each surrounding the next]*; I baked this baby at '350°F for six hours;' I hope that you enjoy its literary flavor.

"Will you be kind, will you be caring? Will you, oh will you, please feed my red herring?"

The Fantastical Adventures Of...

("Buy Me A Sweater?")
(:1:)

Milk ... check. Eggs ... Check. Bread ... Check. Cheese ... Check. Soda ... Check. "Double ... Check." Hey Hunny, I didn't see you there. "Yeah, I just got off work and wanted to surprise you. So, what you got going on?" Well, not too much, just picking up some supplies for tonight's dinner and the rest of the week. How was work? "Not too bad, made some sales and did some paperwork. You know, the daily grind of the middle-wage, middle-American housewife; who also works her tail feathers off because she is just as good as any man, if not better!" Ah, so work was good, that's nice to hear.

So, we got a letter in the mail today regarding a certain someone's birthday party and they are waiting on an RSVP. What should I tell them when we get home? "Well I don't really feel like shackling myself to an answer just yet, we haven't even finished our grocery list." Yeah, I think I'm gonna tell them no too. Hey, do you want to help me pick out laundry soap? We are almost out; though I like the smell of our regular stuff, I have grown tired of it and want to try something new. "Sure."

[Back on the Farm]

"David, did you speak to the Wilkerson's about their party and how we just can't make it, since we have that play to go to this weekend?" No, not yet, but as soon as I get up from my siesta and walk across the hall I'll let them know our answer.

"John ... Hey ... John ... John? ... Hey John Wilkerson, I need to talk to you about something; so please give me a shout back when you get back in. Thanks, Terri."

GOODLOGUE (*PRO*)

In the beginning there was but one man, and he was I. I became me, became myself, became we, which is merely me, upside down; and so starts this chapter in my book, which is also concurrently part of my life. You see, I'm speaking to you from within your own mind. For the words affixed to this page you are reading; yes, this very word itself, is a vessel for me to communicate directly with your mind. You don't know it yet, but are figuring it out as you read this sentence, that I can presently make your mind process, whatever it is I wish you to. Skeedle-deedle-di-do, see how I did that? Keep reading and you will find even more wondrous events to unfold. But this is by far, not a pop-up book, unless it is; and then you must disregard this sentence, except for the part that says to disregard, because that would be circular logic.

What I have to say next, is an assortment of words. And within those words are letters, but not necessarily addressed to any particular person. I have not even licked the stamps. Tell you what, you may lick the stamps for me, and you may also address them accordingly. But do make sure to mail them off before the post office closes, I'm counting on you to do this favor of me. I shall surely pay you back in due time for this generous act you are graciously taking upon yourself, with merit I do add; with merit, indeed! Oh, and if you would be so kind as to pick up some more envylopes while you're at it, I seem to have run dry of them since the last time I spent a life-time piecing together letters to relay a message to others about a grave epidemic that has been sweeping the nation. Like we were all just bunnies made of dust, or something else merely lying about on the floor without so much of a care in the world; except to be afforded the opportunity to do so at our own leisure.

Yes, they are jealous of my talents, why do you ask? Did the fruit juice put you up to this? I mean really, is it such a bother to ask for some sort of consistence in this relationship? I sit here nine times out of ten and just listen to you go on about your day; and the one time I ask a favor of a competent ear that both can keep secrets about my personal life, while at the same time listen to what I have to say … You're almost as bad as the bass on the wall! And they say corn is a better objective listener. Well next time I will just talk to my potato, at least he pays attention to me when I talk. With you, I don't even know where your attention is half the time. Are you even listening now? Look at me!

But I digress, what is in a prologue anyway? Is it a pro at what it does? What does it do, and what does it logue? Is it the rapture of many words finding their way to the surface of the book? Or, maybe, it is a way to capture the attention of the reader so as to take focus off the otherwise uninteresting content of the proceeding pages? I'm not too sure myself. But, perhaps, I can help shed some light on these questions, and more, as we continue to talk about what has been going on. So tell me, how was your day? Did you get to watch the game? I heard it was very well played. They say you came in this morn-

ing with a cold, toward the front … Or were it somewhere near the back? Oh well, we will find out soon
enough, now bend over and cough … I need just enough
time to warm up my thermometer before I take your shot
record out, and shock you with the results of this test you
took. Twenty-ith percent tile is never going to cover the
job, not even half of it…

This is where I make my music happen. Have you
ever been there, that one time, when he said it would always remain the same? That nothing would ever come
between you and him? I have, and I will tell you that it
never feels like it will ever get better than that. And
when you're calm, collective, and ready for bed, it hits
you; you don't even know where you are. Why don't you
know where you are? Have you been drugged?!? Have
you been jogging?!? Have you mistaken yourself for
what you thought you were too good to be? And fur-
thermore, why is it called red velvet? I certainly
wouldn't eat such nonsense. Velvet is fabric! And although fabric may be yummy to the eyes for some, it is
not edible; even though it might prove to be eatable! Or
so says science…

Well, perhaps, I shall go against the laws of logic and
proclaim to eat some velvet, digest its sweet, nectary
goodness; and even write a book about it. I shall call it a
digest, *A Digest Of Velvety Proportions* … And that, my
friends, is this book…

No, clearly I am kidding about that last part, this book
is titled something else; but I haven't figured out what,
quite yet; although some of the content may be similar.
Maybe once I read the rest of it, the title shall show itself
to me, then to you; unless you are blind. And although I
have had the urgent need, and capability, to speak braille;
I have yet the technology to implement it into this book,
but let me try. Bumps aside, and damn those bumps, I
will try this; even if it kills me!

```
      DOT                 DOT
      DOT  DOT  DOT             DOT  DOT
DOT                                  DOT

      DOT  DOT  DOT  DOT  DOT  DOT
                     DOT       DOT
      DOT  DOT            DOT  DOT  DOT

DOT        DOT  DOT  DOT            DOT
                          DOT  DOT
           DOT

      DOT                 DOT       DOT
DOT                  DOT  DOT  DOT
DOT             DOT       DOT

      DOT       DOT
      DOT       DOT  DOT  DOT
      DOT       DOT       DOT
```

Look, I don't expect you to understand what I just braillized, unless you are blind of course. But then, how would you be able to know where I have placed the bumps? "Hidden in plain sight" you might say? Believe you me, these Easter eggs are definitely visible. But that is an interesting question, how do you know where the bumps are lain?

Wait-Wait-Wait-Wait-Wait! Stop the presses! Where was I just like four hours ago? I remember I was going to tell you this fanciful story of how I accomplished greatness, fell from grace, and then worked my way back up by the sweat of my own brow. But then everything went black, and I fell down this crazy hole in the ground. Like really weird, I can't even describe how awesome it felt to be weightless and motionless, but somehow moving faster than reality; which is so much faster than light. Like seriously, as I was moving while also still, I passed light by as if it was waiting for the bus and I was in a sports car driving beyond the speed limit eating red velvet cake with sun glasses on, just because I can; I was the one wearing sun glasses, not the cake.

As I past light by, I tossed a nickel and said, "It's for the bus fare, and by the way, keep the change!" Then everything stopped. I found myself in the corner of this store. There was an old man buying some milk, but he didn't have enough money to pay for the milk, though he did have half the money available in credits; so with a sword, the cashier cut the milk in half itself, and the old man walked away happy; ½ milk in hand.

I was afraid to ask what the price and routine would be if I were to inquire about skim milk, or even 2%; gosh that sounds like it would be hard to figure out just off the top of my head, especially with a long line behind me. It seems rather dangerous to be near such an artisan of the corner market butcher stop, or whatever you would call such an establishment that employs such techniques to give the customers exactly what they want, and concurrently, only what they can afford.

Staring down the corner marked isles, as I walk the line, there is much to see, and much to do; this is true. But no one understands why I am here, all they do is show me fear. I have come close to talking to them, I have even said hello, but no one ever lifts an eyebrow my direction. You would think that I just don't exist, but then how come I can grab stuff with my fist?!? Perhaps the eyebrow in question is too heavy to lift. Maybe I should give a hand, but will I ever see it again? What if they don't give it back? I would be sad…

[Insert frowny face]

And as fast as all that seemed to go on and happen, I disappeared again and came too in my seat as you found me just now. I was quite confused, considering I had applied for a job at that store, and was on my first week's end; I was going to get paid that night I disappeared again. Now what can I look forward to? I wonder if they have my address...

[Distant looks of question and wonder]

SICKLOGUE (*MONO*)

Watching TV this afternoon, the game was on; I had a sinking feeling that today would be a very productive day. I was seated on the couch, and all of a sudden there was this impulse, a deep yearning to know. A question, of sorts, I could not let go. I turned toward my right, and what did I see; seated on the couch, was my ducky, next to me.

I turned toward my duck, and asked, "Ducky, why do you drink and smoke so much?" An innocent question, I thought. But he did not reply right away, it was almost as if he was not alive. He was in such picturesque stillness that I couldn't tell, for the moment, between him and the plastic variety.

I started to ponder, I started to worry; thoughts came flooding, just like a flurry, into my mind. Does he think me unkind? Or does he think, "How dare he question my habits!?!" or "How does he even know I drink and smoke at all!?!" These imposing thoughts felt like a heavy weight, or a ball, deep inside my head; as they throng and they call. All this was happening as I waited for what felt like forever.

In reality though, it was more like seconds from the asking of my initial question, till Ducky finally turned toward me and let out a solitary "Quack," before turning back toward the TV and finishing the game. I too turned back and finished the game, but was still stuck on what just transpired. He quacked at me, he just quacked at me.

[Frowny faces all around]

Well needless to say, I was taken aback by this, but wouldn't let it get me down. A little about me, I'm in my twenties and I work as a host for a restaurant. Even in my personal life I have to deal with unruly people all day, every day; most of my friends aren't the nicest of people to me. Most of them merely use me for my gifts and kind nature, but they are still my friends; and I'm happy to help a friend in need. So, you see, I was quite used to being treated badly by this point in my life. In fact, I almost expect it.

After the game, I made dinner for the both of us, Chicken ala King; his favorite – because he pictures himself as royalty, I even made him a little crown; similar to the ones you get with feel good meals at King-o-Burgerman's establishment on 102 and 5th. And who am I to kill his dreams? I'm not a murderer; though, I have been known to be a cereal killer from time to time. Hey, the captain has had it in for himself for a while now, and I plan on making him walk his own plank; whether voluntarily, or by force. And don't even get me started about the birds or the bees here; but suffice it to say that in either case, it ends in a milky discharge, and an emptiness of sorts; if not right away, then in a while.

After dinner, I drew him a bath, helped him get into it, and tossed bread crumbs toward him; because he enjoys that sort of thing. It really makes him feel like he was back in the wilds of Alaska, home free, and forever young. Sometimes I can see him tear up when we watch nature shows, but he never lets me know his true feelings; not like today, no, not like today.

We had a real breakthrough this evening. I think we really connected on a different level today, and I feel that we are stronger than ever before. Not a word was spoken of that incident, but we understand each other better; I think.

After his bath, I got him ready for bed, and tucked him in; then read him a bed time story to put him to sleep – the one about Ms. Bo-Peep, and how she both lost, and found, her sheep. It is a riveting tale of loss, pain, suffering, joy, and reconnection. I myself went right to bed soon thereafter. But nothing could prepare me for what would happen tomorrow...

SECONDLOGUE (*DUCE*)

As it turns out, tomorrow is nothing like yesterday, well written and set in stone. No, tomorrow is more like a sketched drawing in the water skin of a placid lake. Though you may have the ideas, the visions, even the concrete picture of what tomorrow is, or could be; the image will not stick around longer than your fingers can keep it in that water skin. Tomorrow is an unattainable construction of the mind, and through living in the current "Now," we can possibly obtain the permits required to procure zone perimeters and make this project a success. Yeah! Go team! *[Excited happy face]*

But, *[Frowny face]*, bureaucratical red tape of your own mind will hold you back. Unless, of course, you purchase my patented mind scissors; guaranteed to take care of that unwanted "Tied-up" feeling. No longer must you worry whether you will be halted by the policies of your own mind when you want to do something that the rest of yourself would consider fun and enjoyable. No longer do you have to wait the "Recommended" or "Required" fifteen to forty-five days any longer. No policies hold you back, you say? Then why are you not doing what your heart desires? Trust me, you know that feeling; you're at an ice skating rink, nothing fancy going on there, unless you're wearing a fancy suit. And believe you me, there are reasons to wear one. Why, even now I'm thinking of a few.

But you are nonetheless there, and you notice a girl. She's looking quite fancy to you, and you notice also that she's skating alone; "For shame," you think. "Why is no one there to keep her company?" Well, you figure, why not yourself? Why not, indeed? Don't worry ladies, this could also happen to you, however, I'm only going to fo-

cus on the males at this point since they are most disad-
vantaged ... Then it hits you, the bureaucratical red tape
of your own mind is there to stop you in your tracks.
And the beautiful girl is again left to skate alone. It's an
ever snow balling story of one-sided romancistic pseudo-
love that never could be; all because you were thwarted
by your own worst enemy.

"How does this happen, and how can I stop it?" You
ask? Well, just dial my number in the back of this cata-
logue and one of our operators will gladly assist you in
your purchases. *[Lowers voice]* "Gladly assist you, indeed ... Yep, yep, yep, gladly assist you, indeed. *[Nor-
mal tone]* Gretchen, turn the recorder off and go get my
golf bag; I'm done with this commercial, and ready to
tee-off with Jensens."

Okay, so I see there are some of you shaking your
head at me and saying that, "That never happens to me,
I'm totally popular and everyone loves me." Good for
you, you don't need my help; then why did you pick up
this self-help book? Oh, right, to help yourself ... So you
think you are too good to need my help huh? Well go on,
help yourself then! Do it! ...

I have been living life all wrong, all this time. You
see, I have had an e-pif-a-knee, e-piph-a-knee, y-poof-a-
ni ... e piff-a nee, per knee? ... However you spell it, go
ahead and check, I'll wait...

INTERMISSION

[PAGE INTENTIONALLY LEFT BLANK]

Give us yo minds

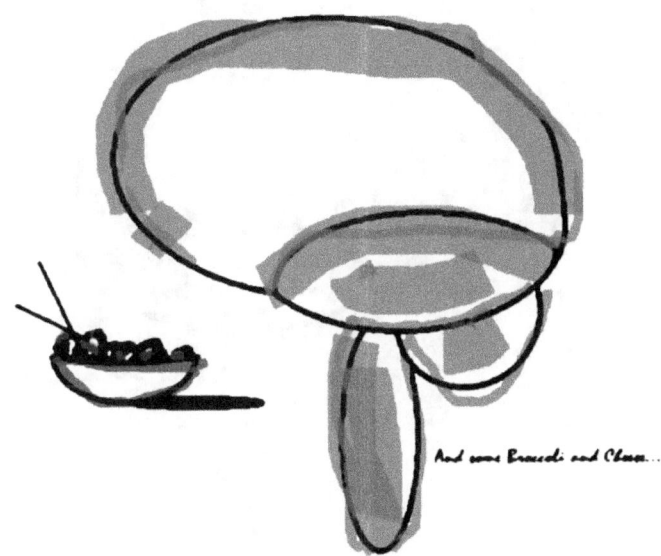

And some Broccoli and Cheese...

Slather it up, and we'll make them say...

Please!!!

[PAGE INTENTIONALLY LEFT BLANK]

Color Blind

But Eye Can C
(:2:)

➢ Hello everyone and welcome to my world. You may only spend a short time here, but I will do my best to ensure it is by far the single most enthusiastic short time you ever thought you spent; within another's mind. Visiting hours may be extended for those willing to endure the extended time ... Those willing to end this tour early may do so, but there is only one way in and one way out. You will have to continue down the path you're on in the order you reside. It's a small price to pay for the freedom to not have to think for yourself ... A utopia, as it were, where there are limitless possibilities for fun and only one rule ... The governing body is in full control and what is said by said body goes ... There is a swing set to the left, a water slide and pool to the right ... Straight ahead there are basketball courts and tennis courts ... There is a 5-star restaurant on the premises and the cooks make anything to order. Anything you want to eat, merely ask and it will appear shortly at the pickup window ...

Pollution? No, everything here is recycled, reused, or otherwise reincorporated to minimize or otherwise eliminate waste of any kind ... Where will you stay? Well of course, we are almost there, that is the last stop on the tour; let me first introduce you to our staff. Col. Baker, an all-star chef of his day, he can prepare and cook any dish conceivable; there isn't a pallet he can't please, or a person he has met that would refuse his service. Ms. Hondurass, the most remarkable of gymnasts; there is no finer person in the sports and health fields, any question or issue, consult her and you will have your answers...

> Physics states that a rolling stone gathers no moss right? Well, it appears that those snooty self-absorbed snobs over at Rolling Stone High School seem to think they are too good to gather moss with the rest of us. It's part of our District-Wide Research Study over the effects of light, moisture, and other climatory factors on moss growth. Who do they think they are!?! ...

> Hey, I just wanted to apologize for how I was acting before. I've been under a lot of stress with family issues and other things. Yes, I know that's no excuse. I just wanted to tell you that I don't really have many people I trust to talk about my stresses. I understand if you are angry with me or don't want to talk anymore. But it would be nice if you still do; and still want to get to know me more. Have a good day/evening/night...

> Epic ... battles, tattles, tails, wails, waddles, whales, rubber ducky, plastic shovel, tin-type pails ... You cannot stop pop, your morning corn ... Not until the victory horn ... One step, two step, three step, four ... How many steps 'till I'm out the door? ... Fe Fi Foe Fum ... I think I just stepped in some bubble gum...

> Show me that sparkle ... All I see is pain in your eyes, you put on a disguise ... No one sees in ... Nothing gets out...

➢ Hi, Zen-Burg, your Prince-of-Pals stated that you may know the location, or the speed … But you may not know both at the same time for any given electron in the cloud … But, shh, don't say that out loud. Wait a minute; does this also go for other things? Like if I were to speed, could I mask my location? Or if they knew where I was, could I mask my speed? Trippy are the things we cannot see … Trippier still, are those we do not know! … For as the clock strikes one, the rest will flee, but it does not have a gun…

➢ For every action, there is an equal, but opposite reaction … For when the apple fell to the ground, his understanding rose in kind … Do you grasp the gravity of this situation? Newtonian Ideologies … Space logic is more transparent … Where there is no tangible matter, reality holds no weight … Circles are king, and with them comes the thinking they are named for. Gravity … Force exerted onto, and by matter, but does it? Magneto-effect … Polar opposites wiz past each other at unbelievable speeds, or is that unconceivable? I mean, it has been specified that if you know where it is, you can't attest to its speed … Immeasurable unless location isn't relevant, as I just stated … Though some must believe it, or else why bother to measure? But all the real-estate agents will tell you, location, location, location … Even Newton can attest to that simple fact…

➢ To have my words forever inscribed on paper … Ha, solve that contraction! … For the paper my words are written on will one day turn to peat moss, and then coal … and my words themselves to oil … Then fuel … For something mechanical … But first the mind … But wouldn't that be funny, if, In 100,000 years-ish … The words I have written, that you have read, were broken down as described … Refined … And the drops of oil, that was once blood, were used in a machine that changed the world somehow? My words CAN make a difference ... If not now, one day they will ... Maybe...

➢ I have been secretly piecing together random pieces of words ... Just like Dr. Frankenstein, M.D. did body parts ... And I will one day soon create a monstrosity the world will know, fear, hate, and then love ... All in that order ... Mua-ha-ha-ha-ha-ha!!! ... Maybe...

➢ Damn bro ... I am insane! ... But I think I'm just the kinda crazy this plan needs to succeed ... But why didn't you tell me? ... Shh, I know, you tried but I didn't listen, I never listen ... It's ok, my ears are wide awake now, and they see what must be done...

➢ Yin-Yang, the unbreakable bond ... You can't exist without your polar opposite ... But if you're on your own ... Then you need no one ... But then you feel alone, yet positive ... So try as you might, to find who you need, You can't ... For you are it ... But you can't see yourself, if you know how fast you're going ... Mirrors don't count bro! ... The reflection in the shadows reveals who we are ... On the inside ... We are constantly on a course to annihilate ourselves ... "Opposites attract" ... "Completing someone" ... Bro the lines are in the sand ... I know what I must do ... It's what I have always known ... And at least this time, no bologna will be harmed ... That! My friend; is a promise! And one I will keep :')...

[smiley face, tear drop]

➢ Get all the ideas and put them on paper, just before you know it, you have yourself a caper ... Then there goes the press, and now they have an angle ... Quickly grab your hat and coat, and try not to dangle ... We must be off, skip town and toss the lamb ... For this get away, in sports car we will travel, Sam ... The quickest way, the furthest mile ... We will be sure to always travel in style ... So say hi to your potted noose ... I'm flying high on my lanyard goose...

➤ I'm Ron, yes I con … But only because I can … You can start anywhere, anywhere but here … There is much to be done, but nowhere to go, and no one to save … So let the day waste away as we sit and stroke the fires … Refill them with tires … And have ourselves a wonderful time at the ball game … We got in for free with a flash of wet tea … "Earl Grey is Oolong," said she, "Mmm, I know I want me an English Breakfast." …

➤ Retrosymbolation … The nation will be run to the blood stone, then run dry … You will be there to witness the ultimate mastery and power … The terrific dynamic that is he … But only for the hour…

➤ Inward struggles leave turmoil outside … Pages and pages turn, just to hide … No one is running to be by your side … When the only thing you have left is your pride … You think you can let go, you think you can survive … You think, that because you can think, that you are alive … But look all around you, and even within, no one is there … Not even your reflection…

➤ Christmas in Hawaii

o   "Oh, the weather outside is delightful. Even way past night fall … 'Round here it doesn't snow. So off to the beach I will go." …

➤ Wheels a turning … Life is a burning … And fading away … I cannot go on, not in this time or day … Can you see? … Right through me? I can … Like a window sill … I'm waiting still … For the right time, or place … Someday soon I may see your face … There is no fare place to go … No boat I can row … I'm headed up stream and I ran out of paddles … There are no more tails or tattles … I forget, but don't you owe me a coke? For long ago we both were caught in a joke … But that makes no sense … There is only one place I've never had to pay rents … Home, they say, is where the hat is lain … But I do not wear things of such to cover my brain … Gotta let it breathe, gotta grasp fresh air through these tentacles that resemble hair ... I can't reach the top of this mountain plane, I can't go on, nor go insane ... Fortunate wonders bespeak up to bare witness to unstoppable thoughts ... To be careful to understand what is within the possible ... But under this feeble misspeak of imagination there is a slight truth ... There is reason beyond the unreasonable ... The engine turns fast, but the wheels spin slowly ... Too much torque, too much inertia? Where can one find solace in a place so chaotic and filled with enemies at every turn? ... Ones that resemble the cause, ones that resemble the side of those on our side? Can someone really believe that there is only one side that can claim victory in this battle? Can only one side be right? What of the looking glass? What of the tin horses that beg to be let free? Can you really sit there and deny the dreams of those fallen? ...

➢ Frost bite the hand that feeds you are just one hand washes the other side is darker than that, I said I wanted my bread toasted mini wheat bread sandwiches are healthier for you will never see what is in store for you if your eyes are closed, we will be back tomorrow...

➢ Frost gate ... Perpetuate ... The unbelievable constant retrieval of the unicorn within us all ... There is a waterfall ... Beyond the rocks ... Don't forget to wear clean socks ... but you can't deny, the power of a lullaby ... Twice is enough, but three times bring charm ... Don't look too hard, you may bring harm ... To yourself, or others around you ... But sometimes there's reason to paint a room blue ... Because the bottom line is, there is only one in this world that can cure all the problems you find ... The ones you encounter, and the ones you leave behind...

➢ Pocket full of poses, staring me down ... I look around the room, and feel faint, so I sit down ... Two days pass, I wake up ... No one is around me, there is only a cup ... "What big eyes you have," did the cup say to me. "All the better to see you with," I replied promptly. And on ward, our conversation ventured ... Vastly traveled, our words would be ... Until one afternoon, the cup had said to me, "I must be going." I was puzzled, and quite scared ... You see, I was alone without him, and couldn't quite figure out what to do. Should I request him longer by my side? Should I pull the covers and attempt to hide? From the world that has played this game for too long, and has been winning this whole time ... Perhaps I shall forbid the cup from leaving me, it's just a cup after all and can't move about by its own free will. Or can it? How did it get there anyhow? Looking more closely, I fear, gave enough time for the cup to make its escape. For as my eyes readjusted to the dimming light of the setting sun, this cup that kept me entertained for all this time, vanished. And with it, did my freedom. "Now what shall I do?" I openly asked myself. "What shall I try to entertain myself with this time?" Then the shadows came to play. And with them, the puppet master, of sorts. But that is a different story, for a different time...

➢ Organizing ... Calculating ... Instigating ... Manipulating ... There is only debating ... My overall rating ... Nothing is ever satiating ... Back seat passengers like to drive cars ... But how can I take control, when the vehicle isn't mine ... It's yours...

➢ Pain ... Going insane ... Cannot clear my thoughts, like the sky with rain ... Too much going on, going wrong ... Just like fields of grain ... There is more than enough sewn in to occupy the tilled surface that is my brain ... I keep quiet while you talk away, I just listen ... Just to hear you out ... I bite my tongue, I do not shout ... I calmly rely while on the inside I cry ... Dying slowly ... Agony ensues ... I cannot sing, or I would sing the blues ... But do not worry, I'll be fine ... I'll walk on egg shells; I'll walk on twine ... But no matter what I do, who

I am, or what I do for you ... You'll never be mine ... This much is true...

➢ Chinese scare crow ... The way the birds go ... There was only two left ... The east slept ... The west won ... There once was just a smoking gun ... But now it has gun cancer ... Rust! ... Gun cancer ... You can stop the noise ... You can't stop the funk ... You can't rock when you're listening to punk ... Or can you? A hybrid solution ... Orange peels aint no pollution! ... Candy is dandy ... But liquor is quicker ... Candy cotton picker ... Sewn in jeans ... Mice that clean ... The roughness sweats ... The bed that wets ... It's nervous ... It's tough to choose ... Once you go, you won't lose ... But no one is troubled ... Lives are doubled...

➢ My Heart Is Racing Fast

    o   Taught us and hair ... One wins, one dyes ... But sometimes you can get a tie. A t-shirt is given out and a loser is hailed ... Or is it stoned? In the end, at least, the night is owned ... To run this race, take a seat with kings. You can tell their status by the presence of rings ... Three are heard toward the end. But it's not over, not till she sings ... That song is unmistakable and viscous. You knew, when I told you, that meal would be delicious ... Mmm-mmm good, like soup from a can. Worth two in the bush, but that rock is still in my hand ... "Get rid of it quick, or you'll end up in the joint!" Words of wisdom ... Straight to the point...

➢ Cure

    o   Chronic ... Pain, Is always there, but I don't complain ... The cause is certainly all in my mind. Or is it my brain? ... My eyes and lungs only hurt when I use them ... It's ok, because I only do that sparingly ... One day I will get one of them machines to do all this uselessness for me. Why not right? ... Is it not the luxury of medicine so you don't have to worry about living life if you can do that vicariously through someone, or something else? ... Like a victimless crime, it doesn't hurt anyone; at least not in this lifetime ... Or is it we that cause what's on TV? Furthermore, which station gets the most publicity? ... Guess I'll consult the 700 club, but only after I get smashed at the pub. Then, I will be in the right mood of mind, to not feel the pain. I will be just too blind...

➤ + 1

o   Plus one, just for fun, Two is nice, But twice the price ... Unless that happens to be free. But then, it's that much better for me ... Call me what you will, but if you do, I'll definitely thrill ... Just like a certain chill, up and down your spine. Call me yours; I will call you mine ... However long you want this feeling to last. But don't wait 'till the offer is past ... The fine is dropped, into the slot on the phone, I'm almost home ... A little longer 'till I have to roam. Sometimes it's like I'm that traveling gnome ... But my style is crisper then that, with a taller walk ... And my lips move when I talk. Favorite color is blue. I also know you like it too...

➤ Seen Through

o   Blue cotton, a potato un-rotten, it sees everything it can. Until you silence it into the pan. It knows not what it will be. The corn has ears, but it can't see. Will you do this thing for me? Carry the cross that carries me? For in my future, un-retold, this it must, say I was bold. To be the few, and proud, I was. One is many, in the fuzz. Fortune favors, and carries on. As they march, to their own song...

➤ Sorry ... Isn't Just A Game!

o   In the middle of my mind, I hear you calling ... Telling me to just go blind; then I will see what you want me to be ... Nothing in your life ... They call me closer. They put me under the knife ... Breathe in fast, but not too much to kill ... I almost swallow, but stop until ... The switch is pulled, but not too fast, they have to make this feeling last ... You call me blind, but you're the one who can't see what this game has done to me! ...

> Morning After

　　o　　The sun sets over the mountain tops. I hear the smooth breath of the pop ... I sat it down, not a minute ago. Next I knew, down it would flow ... You ran right by me, so fast I could not see. There was fright in my eyes. As I looked away ... "You can't be serious!" You did hear me say ... Crossing my eyes, and shutter in my voice. "Yes, the lack of sweater was only my choice." ... Warned me you did, just like I was a kid. "It will be cold," you said ... But it didn't get through my head. Who is laughing now? Evening comes and goes ... As the fire glows, the world around it grows colder ... Only to be then fueled by this insignificant flame of sorts ... Pulling from the world the cold and weak, those that flock to it are they themselves of this resemblance at hand...

> I can't take it anymore; all I see is that door. But I can't go through. I won't fit, for it's too small in the hall. I will not be able to leave this place, for my space is run. But this is not a race. The time I will need to under-exceed this limit I have surpassed, will be enormous, if not simply vast! Now physically I'm able ... To fit through this door ... I do it evermore ... Food and amenities await me, just outside ... They are in plain sight, they do not hide ... The problem is not my physique ... But there is a peak ... Where such a blend will have to end, and a confrontation will ensue ... Perhaps I will win this time ... For now there are only two ... "That's right!" ... Said the mirror on the wall ... "Now it is just me and you!" ...

> Ecology ... Is Fantasy

　　o　　Forward to the happenstance ... If you fight me, I will have the last dance ... They never were but what they are ... You cannot drive your boat-like car ... If you know this meaning view ... The tail will be told as true ... In the field that is new, there is but one man left askew ... Into the night they call your name, to bring you forward full of shame ... But that is not all they want to fill ... They will force down just like a pill ... You cannot call them names and such, for if you do that is too much ... You will never be one with them, for they will beat you with a stem ... The cells that break upon your back, will re-formulate and attack ... The name of the game is ship, battle ... For it all started in, I think, Seattle ... The number on the wall of course, is the picture of my horse ... The title of Ed, was "Mr." son ... And now that horse is all but done ... You ran the derby once too long, for if you call me with the gong; I will not be short with you there ... You will breathe green soup in the air ... They cannot keep you much past eight, for if you go onto your date, the sheriff comes in at 9 ... And his temper is mighty fine ... They will arrest you by 10 o'clock ... Just in time to hear that knock ... At the door you bolt out fast ... They will not catch you, at last ... The end of days is night-fall soon ... I eat cereal with a fork ... Ha-ha-ha, I could have said spoon...

> Leyes

o   In the middle of the crowd I see you standing there, and you appear to reach out to me ... I look into your cold steel-eyes, as if to dream that they were once more real as mine. Then off in the distance I hear it, it calls me to the floor, and I answer back nevermore ... I look whence direction it hath called ... From ... But there is no more a sound ... So I look to where it was to be gone, and I find myself there all along...

> Those that walk with the fire edge of the knife, speak with the pain that they suffered ... You cannot comprehend the sights that are scene when you look past the looking glass, and see the spotted hair run by...

➢ Surprises ... In Your Eye

o   I sit here crying ... Into my milk ... I stand there dying ... Like the elk ... Shot him I did ... With the 45 ... Revolver a kid ... Stay alive ... Just amid ... The crowd...

➢ I can't control the thoughts of you ... Suicide into the blue ... Deep and oceany ... That which is new ... The smell of carpet ... Fresh as the dew ... Life ... As squashed by my shoe ... Is never again ... Sacred like you! ...

➢ Purple ... And Red ... Subtracted, They Make Blue...

o   If a wood were to fall on a log cabin ... And there is no one around ... Would the value of the property ski-rocket due to increased land, Extra room, Newtonian Postulations, etc.? ... Or ... Would the overall value fall, because of some preconceived notion of a person's interest set upon said property, some arbitrary value that someone may or may not pay based upon surrounding properties? ... But you bought that cabin ... Because there were no surrounding properties ... That is the beauty of living in seclusion ... Or so you thought ... Now who is laughing at the low-low price? ... That's right, no one! ... Except the furry forest creatures eating your food ... Since like all things in nature ... Your log cabin, you spent the previous years and pay-checks decking out, has been reclaimed! ... The cycle has been renewed ... Now it is you who will have to fight for your food! ...

➢ Step Inside

o   ... And have a slice ... The cheese is fresh, or so the teller said ... Some sort of block, or is it head? I wonder sometimes if we are the un-sophisticated beasts of burden ... Or were we correct all along? ... And they really did blow up the Liberty? ... That is the statue of sorts ... Only thing we knew were his last retorts ... The dammed-able many ... Over power the damning few

... Man I seem to be caught up in a warp of time ... Or of the mind ... Because in space it's better when you can't see ... What is eating you, may soon be eating me ... Don't make a sound ... "Shh!" I speak, but not too loud ... Only enough to wake the crowd, within your mind ... Cause 20/20 of the hind is the only vision when you go blind ... You look my way and scowl a bit ... I say I'm sorry and I'll quit ... Too late is written above your words ... Suspended there by many birds ... But strange as it were to seem ... How are the birds suspended themselves if not by a tractor beam? ... And if such a device exists ... Why not just use that instead of this plot twist? ... Birds in space ... What a waste! ... Of the latter word I say ... But who is there to hear me anyway? ... Even if you were right next to me ... The words I say, you cannot see! ...

➤ Home ... Alone

o   All by myself ... Sitting alone on top of the shelf ... I dance around when you open the door ... Passing me by, but not anymore ... Or so I think as I look toward the sink ... There are no dishes there, but your hands are not bare ... I wonder why, was it because you have yet to start? Or was it due to the piled Styrofoam of art ... Stacked somewhat high? ... From my vantage I see ... There seems to be a label fixed that's foreign to me ... Wait a minute! ... A vision is heard ... Is that some sort of Chinese word? Take-out is what you had in mind? I thought that's what I heard, but I assumed you would be kind ... Instead you should have taken me out of this cupboard of sorts ... And played a game for sports ... I like the one where you guess the contents of my brain ... I know my label is gone, but it's all the same ... But even if it were strapped tightly to my face ... Would it really be what you taste? ...

He doesn't like to shave

But he loves free food

[PAGE INTENTIONALLY LEFT BLANK]

Ducky: The Unfowlable Fowl.

(An "Irish Setter" Story)
(:3:)

➢ Eulogy
   o   Psychotic as can be ... The symptom is all in my mind ... They said they would find ... The picture is growing ... But they are going blind! ... The sickness I feel will not let me be ... The hurting of all I feel, is only inside of me ... The meds they prescribe only fuel the need ... The urge to purge and somehow bleed! ... But sadly that is not the case for some ... They don't want me dead ... Merely just past numb! ... If I could feel anything, it is sorrow to become ... The main case between the back of my skull and the tip of my face ... I control, the visions of me, that I can only begin to see ... When my eyes are closed, that's where it begins ... When this race is over ... Let me know who wins! ...
➢ Bloggage ... I Write ... Sometimes
   o   But mostly at night ... So, if you're feeling the urge to read what I purge ... From within the

space between my ears ... Caution now, some of it might cause you tears ... You have been warned! ... So please ... Do enjoy, but remember ... Words are special, they are not a toy! ...

> The Fittest Don't Always Make It

   o   I cry at night ... When I am alone ... Sometimes I wish ... You were home ... My walls are clean, cleared of all ... Not even dust is around to fall! ... The morning dew, I see at last, through pain shut eyes, I strain to be ... Woken up by the living room sea ... I stumble forth, then back again ... Then finally motion toward the end ... The sink I find, is dry as a bone ... Which is comforting as I am home ... A feeling of re-morse, and sadness at hand ... I can no longer stand ... Gripping the sides of the tub I sit ... And look at the writ-ings I drew ... Long ago I have forgotten you ... Finally it seems, I can rest ... But is this all just a test? Later on, I know I will fall ... The reflection tells me I have lost it all ... I cannot go on, living this lie ... There is no one left that knows the story ... At least not anyone that will not think it's boring ... At five past twenty, I should feel alive ... But I'm sitting here just trying to survive...

> Writing To Cure The Pain

   o   ... But what also hurts ... Is my hands, to top off my brain ... An ache of the skull would feel null compared to the pain I feel! The head attached to my body hurts too ... Not just the physical aspect ... But the real one too ... Focus ... Is all I need ... Maybe the words I speak would feel better when I bleed! ... To ease that which I feel in every way ... Would be great, if only for even one day! ...

> Depression ... Is A Dish Best Served To Someone
          Else

   o   I sit here and ponder why and who? ... What I could be when I see you ... I look alone inside myself ... And pick up the glass case I leave on the shelf

... Open it slowly ... Cautious, as always, I am ... Then I know that things could be worse ... Crying inside, I try to hide ... The escaping tears ... They force their way through! ... That lets off a cue ... The flooding begins ... And then no one wins ... So I retreat to the spot by my feet ... And hide my face, because now it's a race! ... I remember the times when I was a boy ... I would sit there and look at a toy ... Those days are dead now ... And I can't just go back ... My mind is on the attack ... The visions flood back! ... Stronger each time, I realize, that things could be different ... Things could be better ... Perhaps I'm only under the weather ... A monsoon season of fears ... Causing most of my tears ... Laughing in spite of my pain ... Is ultimately most of my brain ... Causing the worse of the worse to come third verse ... The unrelenting subjection I'm put through is always present ... Thanks to you! ...

> Nothingness

o Drawing a blank ... I stare at the stake ... What was I standing here for? ... Was I only just a blink of my brain? ... Is this the only state I can feel, pain or nothing so real? ... I hurt inside, I cannot hide, from myself for long ... All I can do is carry on, for as long as my feet agree with my purpose ... But there is no rest for the weary ... Not lest they be dreary! ... And then they can lay ... But there is another way ... To end this sufferable, and spiteful duty ... One must let them see ... The ultimate plan ... Was right there in my hand ... The opposite spectrum of course ... And of course they never knew ... Or how could they do, what I had them? ... Again I knew this was a bad idea ... Never to be revealed till the end of the game! ... But for shame, they would never know the truth ... That they were the ones who were really in charge ... The ones leading this body of a barge ... The cost for everything ... Was nothing too small! ... Seems just right ... All in all! ...

- Can't Do No Wrong … Can't Do No Write
  - To my friends … The end is coming … To my foes … The beginning is almost here … And to those that are caught … Somewhere in-between … I'm sorry to say … That you're like dirt to me … If I were Mr. Clean … Box for box … I hear the socks … They call to me from the line … I sit in my chair and feel my hair … All as it falls on the floor … The stories they tell on the "Boob-tube" of sorts … They make me feel at home … Which is quite ironic cause that's where I watch them … No one is here but me and the gnome … The stories are over, and the light is dim … I turn and face my gnome … He faces me, and now I can see … The beady-eyes that he owns … Deep do they stare, into thin air, but shortly deep within me! … I try to defend his stare to no end! … But soon now he has won … But little did I find out why … He was there all along … His favorite show, of all times and more … Was the show labeled, the gong! …
- Purple … It's The New Blue … If You're Used To Seeing Red All The Time!
  - Stressed to edge … I have to pass the test! … I know I'm the best! … But you never call on me … I raise my hand … I hope to win the vote … But something inside … Knows that will rock the boat … And so I sit back down and ponder nothing till I see … That you have forgotten me! … So that I disappear into the background again … Just like I used to be … And so I look around myself and carve my name on a tree … It's the only way to continue my legacy! …
- Throbbing
  - … Down deep in my … Soul … Robbing … My breath can't get no more … I look … And then I see you … You caught me … And now there are two! … Beats … So low I feel in my shoe … The sickness, I feel … Cannot be true … But somehow … I know just what to do … You ask me, which of me you love? … I tell

you, nothing! ... Less than all the above! ... Stopping me dead ... In between the sentences I spit out ... So much pausing causes me to shout ... "No more!" ... I say, "I am heading out!" ... Nothing left ... So I head for the door ... You stop me ... No, not anymore! ... The neighbors ... Hear us down the street ... What's funny is ... This is all a repeat! ... Of last night ... Except this time it's worse ... Because last night ... I left out the second verse! ... And I ... Have just begun ... Wait ... Don't start to run! ... You started this racket ... And thought it was fun ... Now that I'm leading ... I have almost won! ... Soon this will be over ... Just like the days of the sun! ...

➢ Breaking Down

o ... Myself into little pieces with my mind ... I can't hide anymore, there is no place you won't find ... I have hurt you many times before, and again I will not stop ... The more I try to ease your pain, the more I strain, and the harder it is to top ... I'm hurting now, without you ... You know that you are the one, I never knew how much you meant to me when we would have our fun ... Not until you left that day, and never turned around ... I watched you walk away, into the crowed town ... And off I went to look for you, and almost tracked you down ... The sun was setting on the bay, and out were coming the clowns ... Faster now I strained to find your body in the sea! ... Too late was I, did the preacher tell me. Never again, will I see your face, glaring down at me ... Looking up I crack a smile and glare back cheerily! ... Never more, will those days be ... So till I see you someday soon ... I guess this is sorry! ...

➢ Do You Like Poetry? Well I Dabble Or Two

o ... I sit and wonder, what did I do ... I look around and I notice you ... Staring toward me, burning my desire, almost combusting, I light myself on fire! ... It was more than I could handle, looking into your eyes ... It was more than I could handle ... To my surprise ... The feelings that fill me up, and over-flow my mind, are tricky little feelings ... Yes indeed ... For once they hatch, they must feed! ... Their food of choice you might ask ... Is not physical, but it does wear a mask. I have grown with them, and they with me ... They bury themselves so deepily! ... For once they take your name as theirs ... And put a "For" between the more, prominent feature and décor ... That causes them to force my thoughts ... And change my thinking to the "un-clean" ... For every time I think, they scream! ... And everything they say about you ... Sounds ... Just like a dream! ...

➢ Lily-padus

○ Frogs let them stay out late ... The pads are tied ... But not too tight ... I see them jumping ... Off the high part into the light ... But they disappear from my sight ... I strain to see them ... In the dimness ... Their bodies unite ... With the darkness that is the night ... They cry out ... With silent bliss ... Just like an angel's kiss ... Never there but always felt ... I just know how to make you melt ... The new ways you move ... Make me scream! ... I might just fall or break a seam ... The story happens to end so fast ... Sometimes I have to stop to catch my breath ... A new line is drawn with every wrong ... I feel I have been on this mark for way too long! ... The cris-cross action I speak of keeps the freshness that we reek of ... The staring limbs of the tree we are under ... Cause a shudder that acts like thunder ... Was what was staring real or fake? ... Could be that it is as inanimate as my rake ... Or was there someone watching us? ... Painting a picture with their mind ... Watching us but pretending to be blind ... For the sake of our privacy ... Or is it all just me? ... Maybe I can't be trusted with my own secrets ... My own regrets keep me from talking ... Even to myself ... Perhaps I should just yell all my secrets into the glass jar on the shelf ... It should keep the sanity safe ... Clean, crisp and untainted with wonder ... Or at least not filled with a clouded blunder ... The latest of such would turn the jar gray! ... At least it will be nicer inside then has be all day! ...

➢ Fishies Sleep ... And So Do I ... Maybe I'll Just Go Sleep With Them

o   I'm my own worst enemy ... The captain of my own vessel ... The wave that drowns me and berries me in my own sea ... I can't go on ... Not without you, I'll hold my breath till I turn blue ... The counting down 'till the sun is through ... Is sooner at hand and the moon is new ... There is no light after dark it seems, there is only the sparkle of my dying dreams! ... I no longer care, nor do I dare, ask your forgiveness or even air ... My worries to you ... Or whatever I used to do ... I just sit here pondering the uselessness of the Nu-York Zoo ... The only animals I see are people that run free ... The pointed sticks and the sick games they play ... The way they make you run away ... From reality and worse! ... Soon there with me, my name within the hearse ... Written and posted on pine or more ... Whichever is cheaper and easier to store ... Long term I figure ... Underground is best ... For you know how much I love my rest! ...

➢ Cake Isn't Just For Eating ... Anymore

o   I sit in my dimly lit room ... All that accompanies me, is my half-witted broom ... Ponder the visions at night, does me and the broom do ... We sit there quietly and wait for you ... But you never show, and as far as I know, you never were going too! ... So I sit ... And I look ... I even pick up a book ... The story goes on, seemingly forever, but never more than to the edge of each finite page! ... As the story comes to a close, my body fills with rage! ... This story was not supposed to end, not even on the final page! ... Or so the title suggested ... But just like everything I have ever been told, this is another lie, just like all the rest ... So as with the rest of my life ... I will live it the best ... If only I knew the answers to this ongoing test! ...

➢ The One

   o   I sit inside myself, trying painfully to break free ... This solitude of nothing-ness will not let me be! ... The windows are cracked slightly so I can see ... All the light, so strong it blinds me ... Thrown back I am, deep inside, all the power of this light forces me to hide ... The trouble is, that shows itself ... Is that the light is really nice, it holds back visions of the vice ... Standing in the shadows that are cast ... Finally I see them, there at last ... Off in the distance of my mind, I run and run but I am blind ... The voices calling me send direction and course; the final calling sounded hoarse ... Returning home with the spoils of war ... Staring coldly through the open door, I asked myself, "What was all this for?" Looking back, as if there were more ... I ponder the question asked ... Was I too proud see ... That somewhere out there I was killing no one but me? ...

➢ New Age Musak!

   o   In the sea of hopelessness I found you ... Swimming there ... Alone and in despair! ... You tread water like a dog I thought ... But never not, I sail down to you on my cloud of hope ... And sooner now I toss you a rope ... Cast aside from every one you yell my direction ... Cast aside and thrown out of every election ... The selection was theirs to make ... The selection that provided the opportunity to rake in such a catch ... Unbelievable at best! ... But now I understand the cause for all the duress ... The distance happens to catch me by surprise, as I look into your eyes, I see nothing but the skies ... The reflection of the things that look upon your soul ... The visions of such reoccurrences dance all nice and slow ... The stories I feel, while looking down at you, make my breath turn cold and my skin a light tinge blue ... I enter some room at last and watch the clock slip by ... To the corner bakery, where it yells, "Put your hands sky high!" At first I wonder what went wrong ... And oh what could I do? ... Then I'm snapped back to reality, where I realize I am you! ...

> **NEW BLOG**

o   Style and power, two peas in a pod ... The latter one will mostly jolt your rod! ... The first and foremost of the two ... Is much more opinionated where there are few! ... Main stream, where the current is fast, and travels east ... Or west ... At last, the final bell will toll and cast ... The resting place, and leaving space, I will break my cast ... And offer to you a solution to be, the final stroke of the key ... I will not break my vows you see ... This is the call of the worker ant, the silent plight that no one tells ... The honorary school of yells ... I break my back, through and through, but all I get is more grief from you! ... You call my name and send a thunder ... All the chores and to my blunder, I have missed the simplest of tasks of all ... The one involving kissing your ass! ... Well that one I have saved for last, but sadly for you now, I am all out of spit, so I cannot shine! ... All the while I am kissing that rind ... Staring up at you, as you smile back ... Careful now, or I'm on the attack! ... Up like and elephant, charging for the door ... It's just past three with one more chore ... The clock is ticking, racing me to the car ... I can hear it now calling "On-core!" ... Again I pause to check what I heard ... And all of a sudden I feel this bird ... Right on my shoulder telling me it's time to go ... I motion something swiftly but end up stating, "No!" "Suit yourself," does the birdy say ... In little birdy language I can't understand still to this day. So waving back at the tail, or to the head ... Somehow I got confused, just like a slice of bread ... For once you start cutting corners, there's nothing left to do ... You might as well have eaten fast because now your lunch is through! ...

➤ Poison Cures The Visions We Hide

o   45 minutes from nowhere ... Where is my mind, why do I feel only hair? I look into the mirror and I see you ... You look at the wall and you see me too ... The cross between my eyes I use, to cause a surprise, is exactly what you wanted after all ... Sadistic plans are hatched at hand and used appropriately to the cover of darkness that is sent to the few that know now to use it ... Or bought by those that know where to get it ... The one thing on the mind of those that understand nothing but know everything better than those that understand everything and know nothing ... Yet there are the few that know nothing and everything ... Is yet still to be understood ... They are the most dangerous of all since they have the most power to be observed ... The cover story today, is how do you know where the melting point of the imagination is? For if the melting point of water is 32°F and the boiling point is 212°F ... And about 70% of the body and mind is water ... Would the imagination melt and boil at such temperatures as well? ...

➤ In A Sea Of Hope

o   ... I cannot swim ... The salt I taste confronts my whim ... The visions spy me from on the shore ... The rain I feel is starting to pour ... I cannot breathe, nor speak a drop ... The hill I speak of is at the top ... to get there you must run a mile, turn left at the posted pile ... The river does not run right through ... The sea I speak of is inside you! ...

➤ Objection

o   Into the sky I look sometimes ... Into the sky I speak sometimes ... Into the sky I die sometimes ... Sometimes, I cry! ... When I look into your eyes I know why I'm here ... But when you look into mine, my dear

... All you see is fear! ... The truth to be told is that day old bread is best served cold! ...

➢ Noon Time

    ○   In the middle of the day I speak to the wind and say, to you my dear of yesteryear, I pray that you are safe from harm by the way of my arm ... In the ending story that will be told, I must be strong and show I am bold ... You understand me twice as fast, to hear my voice would be your last ... You look into my cold-dead eyes as you wonder what was the prize ... I hold it upon your head, over easy is too close to bed! ... The sun sets but by the wind, the old man blows a kiss to kin ... The sleepy fellow goes then to bed, bumps his head and dreams till dead! ... Often I speak to kill the silence, but no one sentences me to death! ...

➢ ... New Blog...

    ○   How are you today my friend? ... How are you when times are end? ... You call my name without your voice ... hoarse it is, but that's my choice ... I see your face as I walk by ... The jester smiles and winks an eye ... The clock strikes a beat to pass ... Finally I shut off the gas ... The cloak and dagger will soon be here! ... The time it takes to count to three ... Will idlely be your last key ... "Down with the power!" The mice, they say, "Down with the power of this very day!" ... Into the noise does the wind it blow, out with heat like the cows they crow ... You must be sitting here crying by in your rocking chair ... Don't blame me ... I have no hair! ...

➢ The Wire ... The Power

    ○   If you eat your face off with the mace I spray, from the words I say ... I call your name to hear you bleed! ... You look at me through the eyes I seed ... The story I call up to your face, you hear me once but to your disgrace ... I smack you down with clowning grace! ... Funny bones brake in place! ... For you know not what you must be ... Only what you hear from me! ...

➤ Kicking The Box Upside Its Head
   o   In the eye of the beholder, but the beholder has no eyes ... I look at you without my lips for I am a disguise! ... In the shadows I lurk for food ... I confuse the visions inside my mind ... Before my eyes go blind! ... To eat the weasel that mocks my head ... To block the statute of the dead ... You understand what I cannot, but sit here pondering what I once taught! ...

➤ Click On Me And Then You'll See
   o   In the middle of the day I sit down to play ... You call on me with a twinkle in your eyes. What a cleaver disguise ... I come to you like you knew I would ... Once you see I'm here as fast as I could ... You kife me down, just like the clown you thought I was ... But alas I'm still here. The inner spots that are inside my mind ... The thoughts that leak for you to find ... I cannot, will not ... Speak my mind until you call my name as kind ... The one I love is not my own ... The one that I call to my home ... I call you as I stare at my gnome sitting in my yard, all alone. Well there baby tell me here ... Will you hold close for the year ... My heart I give you now my dear? ...

➤ Jolly Old Saint Nick
   o   I don't see a point in it all ... Point to fall ... All I see is last call ... Last call on my life right now, this point I see is the point toward me ... You call my name in vain at last! ... This time I see is just about past ... The words you speak, fall on deaf ears ... And I now cry little tears ... You fear me now and then again, I fear myself as I call you friend ... Now is the day you will regret ... And let us forget to remember ... That it is not yet December! Those gifts I gave you were not to be opened till I see you again ... So saving myself some repent I tell you twice ... Do not open them ever 'till it freezes with ice! ...

[PAGE INTENTIONALLY LEFT BLANK]

The Longest 10 _____

(... "Wouldn't You Like To Know?")
(:4:)

BADLOGUE (*CON*)

Back already? Good *[happy face]* ... As I was saying; the only certain thing that there ever could be, is the
depth and expanse of uncertainty. You can't go there,
without coming back; just be aware, ninjas are always on
the attack – so change your mode – or dress all in black.
Have a fighting pose, so you can be ready to fight back.
The global economy is a jaded mistress, always on the
lookout for new people to screw; but never one to stay
the night, at least not with me or you!

You think that you know me, "That's impossible, you
are not me ... Are you me?" Well, if you are, then you
must know what I'm thinking right now ... "Pineapple"
... Did I just blow my own mind? Am I talking to myself? There are no quotes on these words, so I must be
saying what's really going on in my mind. Does he
know, that I know, what he will say next? "That was a

delicious meal I just ate." Said my date, that I just ate. By date, I mean the kind from the tree, or possibly, the kind involving trees of wonder. But that too makes one wonder ... What was I talking about again?

They say life is unfair, life is untrue ... How can that be, when life is all you? All you make of it, all you know. All you can find in life or just what shows. Is there an answer within us all; one that begs to finish the question that we all call? There were too many of us asking, too many to say. There will be one left of the impossible day. I walk into the columns, I visit the rows, I seed the ground, I scare off the crows, I'm left to bake in the sun, and I'm forgotten like I am no one. But I'm not affixed to a post, I'm not filled with straw, I am what I used to be, and I still obey the law!

Don't look at me, as if to be afraid. I don't have much power, and I never get paid! What might I be, what might you see? Is there an answer to which you ponder, pander, or wonder for free? Or do you still have to pay the price; perhaps a cost is measured twice, once inside, trying to hide, but now resides right by your side?

PREFACE (*QWAD*)

Waking this morning, I prepared for the day. I got Ducky ready for work; he works at a Chinese-food restaurant as their head chef. After sending him off, I too went about my morning routine. Upon reaching my destination, I exited and locked my vehicle.

Looking around, I had this odd feeling, "This feels too real," I said. "Was it something I ate? ... Or perhaps something I said?" I felt a sickness, a feeling of dread. Perhaps, I thought, it was all in my head. Stopping for the moment, to try to catch my breath; but try as I might, my body felt as though it was under duress. Panic ensues, lights ... Of reds, yellows, and blues ... Flashing toward me fast. I can see it on the news. The day was just past Tuesday, I had just gotten paid, but now it feels like my heart is committing a limb raid! A passage flashes, a vision lost. I would think of you, but at what cost? There once was reason, and melody. Of thoughts of you, there were so many!

Penny for your thoughts, but two cents I do not have! I cannot even afford to call myself a cab, to escape this place, these dreams. Even my personal paradise has streams! No one to turn to, nowhere to run, how can I escape? When was I done having fun? I look at you, all tucked in, in my bed. Recalling the day when that old man bumped his head. It was a peaceful storm, but it was not raining yet! ...

I was at the betting tracks and had just tricked out my horse, but still lost my bet. As I looked on in wonder, I looked also in dread. My heart was racing faster than my horse, and visions were playing inside my head! There were trumpets a-tooting, birds fluttered by. Into the windmill, did the wind cry!

I make the most of my earnings, the most of my time. I make the most of my sentence structure, even when I create sentences that sound similar to each other. It isn't against the law!

Calming down, I notice, I am just fine. I pat myself on the chest, and look around just to see. The world has not changed, not it, nor me! So onward I journey, on this path I have made, and into the building; for I gots to get paid! *[Excited smile and wink]*

[Many hours later; frowny face]

Upon relief of my duties, I clock out on time, and abandon my post; for there is my name on the corner lime. Another time, another day, I will return as head host.

I know that you will miss me, I know that you care. I know you all think of me, when I am not there. My journey continues; there is much work left still to be done.

Climbing back into my car and off I must drive. To my next destination, it's what keeps me alive!

FACE (*SEVN*)

I arrive in the suburbs, at the house of my friend, Tim, and drive up to the gate. I get out of my POS car, and walk past the gate into the house. On my way in, I passed a small yard before entering the front door of the house of my friend, Tim. In and down to the basement I went. Upon reaching the basement door, I heard sounds signifying there was a game of some sorts going on. I entered and took a seat in the empty chair in corner of the poker room, they were playing poker. The room was filled with smoke and dimly lit.

Time and games pass, as I win and lose, till finally I am out of money. "To the ATM I must go" I say; "In order to pay out my debts, this vary day!" Back through the door I went, and up and over to which I first arrived at this house of my friend, Tim; I exit.

This time passing the front yard is different, with expansiveness all around. As I walk toward the gate, *[panning in front]*, a clown is seen, saddened; holding a daisy with only three petals remaining on the stem, while all the rest are floating in a tear puddle on the ground. Though you wouldn't know he was sad, except that his real smile was a frown. But it was not upside down! Seconds thereafter, a bull came charging in from the left, halted only after striking the sad clown; causing an explosion of sparkles and smoke which faded right then after. Seconds more and I appear from the left, unaware of the occurrences that have just happened hence. Though looking over at the bull, I can plainly see the look of anger and demise on his face as he snorts out smoke and sparkles from his nostrils as he hoofs his foot into the ground as if to signify that he is about to charge my direction! Yet, with giddy charm and grace, I interact with the bull and clam him down with a few short pats on his head.

After I finish calming the bull, I go back into my now more expensive car, and head for the city.

Arriving at the ATM of choice, I exit my car and see an old friend and business partner, Wally. Wally and I exchange "Hello's" as I'm about midway from the ATM, a good thirty-forty feet from me. Wally then poses the last question of his life, "What are you doing here?" To which I reply, "Just making a withdrawal." To that, Wally puts his pocket book into his coat pocket and heads for his car; when suddenly I leap into the air, do three kicks, pull out a medium size ball-pein hammer, and lodge the ball side directly into Wally's heart; killing him instantly … At the very moment of impact we see the bull now peacefully grazing where the sad clown once stood; he raises his head and gives off a loud mooish-cry as his body, from the center, bursts into a small blue supernova, but dissipates quickly … Seconds after gathering myself, I reach inside Wally's pocket and retrieve the wallet and money stashed inside.

Saying a few short words of thanks to my now late friend and business partner, I tip him twenty dollars before I jump back into my expensive car and head back to the house of my friend, Tim.

Arriving back to the gate of the house of my friend, Tim; I get out of my expensive car and proceed through the gate onto the pathway to the house. As I'm passing the expansive front yard; now in view, in the place of where the bull was is a very sad crying cow, with the "Moo-hoo-hoo's" to go along with the sad-sad eyes. Like a puppy that's lost its home. I see this and as I'm nearing the cow I place my hand out to pet her on the head, and show her that it's ok; that everything will be alright.

An eternity of time passes between us. Stars and planets; galaxies gather into existence and burn with a furry, the likes of which have never been witnessed by the eyes of man! Until finally all the existence of the world and universe grows black and dissipates; and with it, the sorrow that once flooded the mind and body of the cow. 'Till finally she gains the courage to move on, and head back to the grazing she once enjoyed when she was a kid; in the middle of the front yard, near the giant redwood trees by the far end of the lake.

I then proceed to the front door of the house of my friend, Tim, and inside. Down to the basement once more; only this time it's for payback, and payback shall there be! And as I enter the poker room, they were still playing poker; I reach into my pockets and pull out the last thing my poker buddies will ever see from me again; well, as far as they know! ... *[Insert winky face]*

After taking care of business, I leave the poker room and proceed to exit the house. The path to the gate is much faster reached this time, as the front yard is but again as it was when I first arrived; small and vacant! I arrive at my POS car, get in, and drive off into the sunset; another day, another day! ...

POSTFACE (*PINT*)

I arrive home, and realize it's just past seven-thirty; I have to go pick Ducky up from work. I don't want him to think I'm a jerk. So, off I head to the Chinese-food restaurant, *Miko's Sacred Garden*, and asked Miko if Ducky was still working. I was told, "No, he not here, he peking now!"

I looked at her kind of strange, but shook it off, as I thought I knew what she meant; so off I headed to the local watering hole. I found the place he ventured, and stopped in for a drink myself. "Hey, I'm looking for a small yellow fowl-smelling creature, who answers to the call *[of the wild]*," I said to the bartender. "Over there in the corner, with those two chicks," he said, as he pointed toward a dimly lit booth. I migrated toward that direction, but the place was pretty crowded; and the music was kinda loud. I felt like I had to squawk at Ducky just so he could hear me. "I have come to take you home," I said, as he just glared in my direction before returning his attention to those chicks he was seated between. A few minutes later, he then looked back at me and gestured for me to have a seat with the three of them. I sat, and we talked for a bit, as our tongues wallowed in round after round of drinks.

As the evening was getting late, and towards the end of the conversations; Ducky pulled me to the side and exclaimed, "I think one of these chicks is a swallow!" To which I replied, "Sorry about my fowl language, but Ducky, both of those chicks look like pretty dirty birds, if you ask me! Besides, it's already half past ten, and we both have work tomorrow!"

Returning to the table, both Ducky and I, we ordered a few more drinks from the bar. By this point, the chicks were starting to feel like flying south, as most chicks of their species do. So Ducky hatched a new plan. "Hey, you two wanna come over our place and roost for a bit?" This was just the invitation they were looking for. So we exchanged numbers, and told them that we didn't live too far. They were going to follow us back.

[Ring-ring, telephone style]

"Hey, the place is just up the hill to the left, the gate code is triple-three, twenty-one, spaghetti ... Once you pass through the gate, make a right and park in the first available stall; we'll be waiting in the parking lot for you." "Hey Ducky," I said, "How much were the drinks?" "Don't worry about all that now," he told me, "I told the bartender to put it all on my tab. I'll get my bill in the mail next week ... I told him, 'I would gladly pay you Tuesday.' To which he replied, 'It is Tuesday!' To which I rebutted, 'I meant a different Tuesday!'" And so, there we were, Ducky, Me, and those two chicks. The only thing standing between us was air, or tiny suspended particles of dust, or whatever makes up said dust and things! "I call the bed, you can have the couch," I said, as I ran up the stairs with one of the chicks ... To save you a much longer story and some detail, both of the chicks were swallows! Mine, however, mentioned before our particular encounter that she had a particular set of boobies *[Excited happy face]* ... I shortly realized after, that she was married with two kids. *[Sad face]*

More so when her phone started ringing, and she exclaimed, "Oh shit! My daughter, Raven, is calling me! ... I'm sorry, I have to go home before my husband gets off work ... He is a night owl, you know!" "That's fine," I said, "But before you go, would you care for something to eat?" "Sure," She said, as we both went down stairs, and into the kitchen where I started to cook breakfast. Ducky and the other swallow came into the kitchen as soon as they smelled the food.

We all ate and conversed a little bit longer before the two of them had to go. Upon pushing back from the table, my swallow came over to me, and as she gave me a hug, she said in a provocative tone; "Thank you for breakfast, and for scrambling my eggs just right! *[Wink]*" Then they both turned to walk toward, and out, the door.

Looking at the clock on the wall, I realized the time. Just past six in the morning. "Ducky, we have to go to bed," I stated out loud, "Can't have your fowl temper causing everyone's day to be ruined, just because you didn't get enough sleep, and you have a hangover." So, I drew Ducky a bath, helped him get into it, and recanted the day's adventures to him while he enjoyed the suds as they cleansed and purified his downy nature. He felt much better after that bath, much better indeed. Afterward, I tucked him into bed, and sung him a lullaby to allow him to rest his weary head. I too went to bed as soon as my song was through, good night Ducky, from me to you!

WOODLOGUE (*SIES*)

I find myself running a blind race. I find myself in a relatively dark place. You cannot possibly, be the one that I see! How can you tell that you know me, when you are blind, how can that be? Sitting here, I pull out my hair. All I see is underwear, or under there, that place somewhere. You go at night, you pick a fight, and then you realize that I was right. Two days ago, I picked up some zigzags; I got them from this guy you might know. He is cloaked in secrecy, wherever he might go. He wears a mask, and a hat, dark clothing, two boots. He spells his name with a "Z," and yells, "Oh crap," when he shoots; this is probably why he fights crime with a sword … Moving on with this story, because I can tell that you're bored…

"I can't be too sure, but did you order a movie on the TV today?" The cable box told me that you might have, but it was too distracted by the view outside that it couldn't be too sure itself. I had a talk with our neighbor about what was going on this afternoon, and she assured me that that will not happen again! She said she was sorry that her blouse had fallen on the ground, and that when she bent over to pick it back up, her pants fell down too. It was a strong wind that came between the houses and blew all her clothes off the clothes line, and into the mud. It didn't help that she used inferior clothes pins to secure them!

I told her it would be ok. "That happens often, and it is nothing to be ashamed of." She was relieved at my soft tone, and warm, caring nature. She even invited me in for a drink of lemonade. I accepted her offer and proceeded inside after her. Upon sitting at the dining table, I noticed there were some hotdog buns on the counter by the sink. I asked if she had any hotdogs, to which she shook her head and told me that she was fresh out actually *[Sad face]*, and that she really wished she had some, since she had been thinking of having a hotdog or two that afternoon. "I have a sausage if you would like," I said as I reached into my pocket where I keep it. "That sounds tasty," she replied, *[Smiley face, eyebrow raised]*, and we both enjoyed the afternoon sipping lemonade and watching the sun set...

TRANSMISSION

Arctic Flys Are Cold SOB's

("Sub-Orbital Bug")
(:5:)

➢ Interesting Predicament

    o   Look at my eyes when I shout into your phace! ... You love to hear me scream at you, you stand there with such grace ... I love to hear your cries of pain as I strain to keep a straight face ... And sooner now, we are at my place ... The time is near and I fear that you will be gone soon ... So by the power of the moon, I say to you my dear ... "Let me in, oh, let me near ... The entrance to your bathroom, clear!" ...

➢ Gold Stich

    o   Back on the weasel, hits him with the sauce ... You know Mr. Hanky, you just beat up the boss! ... Into the night they scream, bleeding all their power ... Into the watch-type elemental tower ... You know the status of the king and you know the jester's style ... But no one stands to think that all the while ... When you were sitting there waiting on your time ... You

paused for nary a moment to pick up that loose dime ...
And the time it took to release the hounds ... Was just
enough to open bounds and kill the clowns of the old
country ... That beacon to be in the new order of time
and pestilence to be halted just as it was once before ...
That which calls to the hills to be in the story of the hour!
... And this is why, kids, instead of raw wheat, we use
flower! ...

➢ Orange Blues

o So there I was, standing there staring at
the ground and wondering if I should jump ... And
whether I would hit, or would I miss the writings there ...
Would there be a story told of my bravery, the sight that
could be told by my boldness or of my heroism? ...
Would the neighbors stand there and have their jaws hit
the floor as they watch in amazement to the spectacle I
am about to proclaim as my own? ... And then it hit me, I
had completely forgotten to throw the rock ... Yeah, hop-
scotch is a tough game, 90% mental you know!? ...

➢ Spanky Goes To The Moon

o Look into my book case and tell me what
you see ... Inside the chest of drawers, you will only see
me ... For I bring you words of encouragement and sol-
emn sacrifice ... And to be heard, is an encouraging word
... For the elephant stampedes at midnight ... And the
feeling is left to be alright! ... Once upon a hill top yonder, there stood a boy of mediocre size and stature ... But
nary a fool was he ... For he could handle the tool at best
and sooner than later, you'll get hit in the chest! ...

➢ To-day

o Is a great day in the morning ... But a
wonderful day to be dead ... In the morning, in the morning ... Look into the bright shinny star in the sky ...
Watch out for yourself as it pokes you in the eye! ... In-
ternal bliss is halted by the face, and soon, you will understand why I sing with grace ... She has a beautiful

voice, but it is only by choice that I sit to be had ... And I thank her for that song!...

> Porch

o   You sit here with your coffee cake eyes ... And I can see through your benevolent disguise ... Open your mouth and speak clearly my dear ... You have not eaten one single bite all last year! ...

> Tomorrow's Yesterday

o   Went to bed ... Woke up hit my head ... Had some school with a noodle or two ... Department is fine ... Engine number 69 ... I pass three ducks as they waddle by ... One fourth one resembles a half limped guy ... You call my name but once, not twice ... I answer you as I shoot some dice ... "Seven or eleven," I say as it bounces, "Deuces wild," I hear from the crowd ... Twice it fools me as it states a number 9 ... Soon I hear the answer that was to be mine! ... Sitting on the book shelf there, there was once the sight to care ... You pulled my book from off the ledge ... Sooner than now I will jump that hedge! ...

> Evil

o   Evil beans march up my face! ... Into my mouth with such disgrace! ... They march right up to my brain with power! ... Faster than I could even take a shower! ... One of them proclaims himself king ... He challenges my brain ... Thinking it is a huge bean! ...

> Yesterdays' Tomorrow

o   Woke up ... Silenced my alarm, got up ... Not doing anyone any harm ... I sit down and think to myself what did I do ... In the evening time ... I think of you. Morning has come and gone ... What or whom have I done wrong? ... You leave my bed side to answer the phone ... But no one has called, soon there will be no one home ... Sad I am when I know the truth, Though you lied right through your tooth! ... Rested are my inhibitions, not warranted are my traditions ... I gave to you what you did want ... But now you sit there and strut to flaunt! ... So back I stay from out the crowd, I give you your space ... So, I hope you're proud! ...

➤ Today

  ○ Woke up ... At 4 ... Got up ... At 5 ... Still don't feel alive ... Went for a swim ... But did not have the whim ... To jump into the water ... I just didn't feel like getting wet ... At least, not yet! ...

➤ Noon Kine Fun

  ○ Into the night I see the bright-bright sun ... Standing softly I sit there as I wait for her to see ... What, oh what is steadily calling me? Into the rain is the wind sock of my dreams ... And the custard calls me "Sweetness!" As it floats away on buttered wings! ...

➤ Enter dogma

  ○ Enter the night, cold but bright ... The one that is head fast and strong to be the one on the hill top yonder ... Shall forever proclaim that this land surveyed to be in the grips of those that so hold it ... In the title of this day and to this day it shall be his and his alone! ... Into the light with undying evil that shall call the darkness home ... For only the shadows shall cross the span that is dusk and shall emerge unharmed toward the field that has shown itself toward dawn! ... There is but a boy in the afterglow of the sun that shall show himself to be known as the one that shall shave the town of its whales! ... And then shall hail into the next timeframe and call to the roasted host of the fair land that is to be in the knight of the round ... But the collared few that is in the calling of the evil that rests to be in the land aforementioned to be possessed by the one that is true in the heart of men ... But not into the beast of burden that which shall be called upon in dire times ... As to be used for the good of which it is to be called good at all...

➢ In Dependence

o   Happy fourth, but I'm fourth from happy … Our newspaper clown just smacked my pappy … Down the street I heard him run … Those silly shoes must weight a ton … Two steps back and one to the front … Boy wasn't that pick up line blunt? … You told her off, and then to get into the car … Good thing for you this was at a bar! … I sit down beside myself and ponder my vary existence … I look to my left and see myself looking at me quite distant! … Into the night they call unto the light, within his mighty hands there lies the plans … To go to the east and fight off the yeast … Rising in the west, but at best it shall be a tie! … For to win would be good … But to lose as it should, would be bad … But not worse than to win while your head is still in the noose! …

➢ Twinkle

o   Twinkle-twinkle little star … Are you there, or in the car? Will you answer my invitation from the nation of Fudd? And when you call me, will you be my bud? You tell me lies without a thought of compromise, and I sit here staring softly, deeply, into your eyes … "Hold me close," you say as you see my arms surrender … Love me deeply, hard and tender! … I'm thrown back, poised I was with the notion of attack … But now I see there couldn't be, anything worse than what's on TV … Unless, again, I'm caught up in another layer of your web of lies! …

… !seil fo bew ruoy fo reyal rehtona ni pu thguac m'I ,niaga ,sselnU … VT no s'tahw naht esrow gnihtyna ,eb t'ndluoc ereht ees I won tuB … kcatta fo noiton eht htiw saw I desiop ,kcab nworht m'I … !rednet dna drah ,ylpeed em evoL … rednerrus smra ym ees uoy sa yas uoy ",esolc em dloH" … seye ruoy otni ,ylpeed ,yltfos gnirats ereh tis I dna ,esimorpmoc fo thguoht a tuohtiw seil em llet uoY ?dub ym eb uoy lliw ,em llac uoy nehw dnA ?dduF fo noitan eht morf noitativni ym rewsna uoy

lliW ?rac eht ni ro ,ereht uoy erA ... rats elttil elkniwt-
                                                    elkniwT
                                                    elkniwT

➢ Read Me Like A Chinese Book

○   Looking deeply into your eyes ... You once noticed a faint surprise ... The door knob clatters, a clickity-clack ... Inch by inch, the lights go black! ... Faster now your pulse, it quickens! ... Deeper now, my gaze it thickens! ... The time is nearing, but you're not fearing ... I'm almost finished, I can smell is searing ... The steak from the night before, cool to the touch up top the floor ... You're singing me a little tune, same as before, way back in June! ...

➢ Eat Your Own Phace

○   In the middle of the night, I can hear them calling ... Calling my name to stand up to them ... Inside my own mind I can see them ... Closer the more I blink ... And soon the hour is upon me ... Into the night I step, latched and ready ... For now is the time I have waited for so long, now is the order to go ... To fight and stand fast ... To accept the fate that which hath beckoned me to be here is now shown itself to be! ... And all along it was really deep within me! ... The answer that I have been searching for, all that much and even more! ... I look to my right, I see you ... You look to your right, you see me too ... And what are we left with is but nothing to do ... Into the mirror I do sing, and when I think of you, I remember my ring ... The one I gave you, now doesn't mean a thing! ...

➢ Un, Mi Bologna

○   I stand here in the living room just about to grab my broom ... And in to the floor I see ... Watching me is my bologna ... Sitting there it peers my direction ... Pure perfection of this meat selection duth yield a sort of self-discovery ... But along comes a turtle out from her girdle! ... And into the path of my gaze ... Like shooting ducks in a maze ... You cannot be too careful, or too wise! ... All you have to do is close your eyes ... Ha-ha, that's what they want you to think! ... But really my friends, the answer is in the sink ... For the water is what the turtle is after ... Stealing your bologna only brought him laughter! ... The true villain is you ... You know who you are, and you know it by far! ... You are the best of the best ... But you haven't past the final test ... You have to go far, and few go the furthest, than General Sir McWilliams P. Ernest! ... You see, there once was a man that flew near the coast ... But he was never seen after his first big boast! ... That he could fly half way to the moon ... He would be back half-way past in June ... But something caught his eye on the track, kept 'ol soldier boy from ever coming back! ... You know what I'm saying, you know of this noise ... You keep on playing with all of your boys! ... But you never stop to think of the way that it toys ... With my heart! ... Into the night I see your face ... And then I feel like giving an embrace ... But stopped am I ... And no feelings protrude! ... For I would not want to be halted by someone so rude! ... You have stopped me before and threw your hands toward the door ... I looked that way sadly and asked you for more ... Hinting at me, that time is almost up, you toss my things at the pup! ... Sitting there near my truck ... All I wanted was a little more luck! ...

> You Don't Know Me

o   You only think you do ... What you cannot see, is that those three little words come so easily to me! ... I'm a literary poet, but you didn't know it, all you knew was the same thing I told you, over and over ... 'Till you got bored ... Told me it was through and showed me the door ... I walked, out not because you wanted me to! ... Mostly I was done and am through! ... I am moving on in my life ... Maybe have some kids with my wife! ... You don't care about me anymore ... All you want is what is fresh, and something to score! ... I have pity on you, your family, but who cares about me ... I got my car fixed, and guess what, it was free! ... You call me names and lie about things ... You still tell me those words, and then my ear rings! ...

> Bullets Cascade *[Mood: Apathetic]*
   o   ... Through the briny sea that is my brain ... I shot them there just to feel the pain ... Said pain, you say, I have caused yourself every day! ... And now I see that you were right ... But I can't see you ... All I see is night ... At the end of it all, I feel I'm starting to fall! ... The ground comes up to meet my body, intertwined at last we are ... Forever joined and bound to boot ... Sooner now my body with be soot! ... And as I fall, I hear your voice ... But laughter follows with a bit of praise ... As you raise your hands and clap aloud, then around you there assembles the crowd ... They jauntier and whistle ... Hoop, holler, and yell! ... They want you to say what you did, they want you to tell ... The destruction you caused me, the pain that I felt! ... The never-ending guilt that you dealt ... Done am I now, done with it all! ... Be there a rose for where I fall? ... One that is black and blue! ... The color of my heart left by you! ...

> Just A Dog
   o   Looking for a bone ... No place left to call a home ... Will you not take me into your heart? Some place warm, just for a start? ... I look at you, you look at me ... I know just what you want to be ... You call my name in the cold at night ... Right after we had our fight ... And in the morning time, you wake me up and we start to chime ... News is good, and news is bad ... Oh what fun I thought we had! ... Again you look around yourself, and you notice your picture on my shelf ... The caption is not there! ... And you realize I am nowhere! ... You look around the house for me, outside and in the street ... My car is gone and so am I ... You are mad that

I didn't say goodbye! ... But alas, I will be back ... With all my love and a snack! ...

> False Allegiance

o   I call your name in the middle of the night ... For you are the one that I fight, not for power or for money at best ... I fight for you, for all the rest! ... You say you love me, but I cannot see ... The love you say you have given for free ... This fake smile that protrudes from within my soul ... Is not real, it is not at all! ... You convince me all the time that you are true ... That there is not anyone that could do the things that I make you think of when I'm without you ... But when I turn around there is a mime clowning ... Turning my upside-down frown, back upside-down ... And now I'm left here touched and bewildered at the slightest insignificant blunder ... And I do wonder! ... "What would there be without me?" Could there be happiness, would there be sad? Could just everyone adopt a system of glad? ... Content and proper is the days of yore! ... Old as the English, but half of the bore ... You look unto my cold-dead eyes, like the time it was long ago ... You know the one I'm talking about! ... The one with more shout, less bounce ... But just a smidgen of heart-ache, with plenty of pounce ... The mind is a beautiful conundrum of possibilities to speak of without words! ... But you can always express oneself with a song that sings its own lullaby ... One that might even make you cry. A hint of bourbon on your lips as you quip my tongue ... And tell me that I'm wrong, but it's really just a damn good song! ... The bourbon quickly gets replaced, but not before your face gets maced! ... Sooner than later now ... I fed some whiskey to my cow ... Sour milk was what I then had ... Now I have curds and whiskey, but I'm not mad ... I sell it on the market for a buck or two ... Double over the competition of sorts ... They call this one a major league sport ... Don't look at me, says the image in the mirror ... I reply, "Do not act so queer! ... You know your stance, and you stand it just-ly, but just to be quite thrustly ... You could prove to be rusty!" ...

> Love Me ... My Dear

  o   You look at me, and I begin to tear ... A faint softness is at my embrace ... The true calling of the night is a waist ... If only I could have known ... You call my name and smile from ear to ear ... I let out a faint ... "I love you my dear" ... You look away and then start to wonder ... At last, there on the hill top yonder ... In the cold of the evening I see what I should! ... But I know not now what I would ... "If the time it takes to cut the tree down, is also the time it takes to dress a wee-clown, then the day is mine!" ... Said the red tri-corner hat ... Three bills a plenty is too much for me, too rich for my blood kind sir ... But beg of me not, for I own the pot, and you shall play till you die if you wish ... But dare as I say it, shall no one be played yet ... At least not until drinks are done ... And then the merriment! ... And they carried yet three bags of fun ... In the first was yel-low stuff that looked kinda sweet ... "Good enough to eat!" Said the fat man, who knows a thing or two ... The second bag had chocolate, and the fat man knew just what he should do! ... So grabbing up the third bag with one hand on two ... The fat little overweight man gripped upon his shoes ... And when the story came about, that no one caught the news ... That even though boys will be men ... They often forget to tie their shoes ... And that is a moral that will clearly sing the blues! ...

> A Little Antsy In The Pantsy *[Mood:*
              Confused]

  o   I feel like drinking my ******* life away, all cause of things you say! ... I can't tell the truth from what I see ... All I know is what you're telling me ... Know this and be halted ... I know all and understand most! ... You can fool my eyes but just do not boast! ...

Because in the end, it might be your roast ... I believe your lies! ... I do not even know why you try ... I would not be as hurt If I only knew the truth! ... Why do I have the feeling I need to hire a sleuth? ... I really wish I didn't have these feelings toward you! ... I really have never lied to you ... But I do apologize! ... Look deeply into my eyes ... I have been telling you the truth all along ... But you just skipped about to your very own song! ... Singing me bits and pieces as you please ... Whatever would bring me to my knees! ... Well, now that you have me here my dear ... Tell me what I want to hear ... What I have been asking you for all along ... The truth behind your fancy song! ...

- Lies
  - You lied to me for so long, that I can't understand your song ... You tell me you're picky, and you like him, 'tis true ... But you say you aint done him and he has not done you ... You spend your time like you're joined at the hip! ... Watch out closely, because you just might slip ... One false move, and your hips could be joined ... Much more closely, and more in-groined ... Maybe it was me that pushed you there ... Maybe it was me that caused my own share of this which is happening ... But you know what? ... I have not lied to you, why are you still lying? ... All I want is the truth and sorts ... Tell me who is a better sport? ... You know this has happened before ... I once knew a girl that did me and a friend ... And you know what in the end? ... Me and my friend found out the truth ... But it was not by her ... It was me and him at the corner counting out the ways she played us both ... Having her ways with us as she wanted ... And how she jaunted back and forth! ... Now I'm sick in the stomach feeling like I have been lied to even worse than before! ... You tell me you love me ... Only me... And you only want to be with me! ... You say baby is for those you love ... And babe is just a name you use ... So

why do you use baby for him? ... And a heart with both names in it? Please just tell me what is really going on ... So I can change my radio dial ... Because I'm done listening to the same old song! ...

➤ A Betrayal *[Mood: Irritated]*

○   "Hello," I say as you pass me by ... To my surprise you put up your disguise! ... I can see it all so clearly now ... Comments here, and comments there ... You pretend to have some compassion when I ask you for action ... I ask for the truth, but all I get is lies ... It is spelled for me in secret numbered spies! ... You play these games with my heart, and you taunt me to break apart ... The thing I have had for a while ... But I would do it all for you and with a smile! ... But now I'm lost and without a trace ... You might as well just spray me with mace! ... At least then I would have a different pain to think of ... A different pain to speak of! ... How could I not see the truth? ... I know I felt it ... But you lied through your tooth! ... Now I'm a second fiddle! ... One who only knows one riddle ... But I can't even call your name without being put through a sea of blame! ... You call my number and cut me out ... Then you want me to sit there and shout ... You want me here, and you want me there ... But you have him, with must despair ... I say these words aloud and softly ... I would not want you to not want me! ...

➤ Chinese Sunday ... Is Really Monday!

○   So there I was, walking again down the path so few take ... And I looked at myself in the reflection on the floor ... What am I doing with my life to make it such a bore? I understand I have no friends, no one that brings a means to this end ... But when I wake up every day, I wonder what my life would be like anyway ... Without everyday being rainy and painful ... I ask that you will pull my head out and wring the blood dry ... Before I cry myself to sleep tonight! ... By "You," of course, I mean me! ... For that is only who I see! ...

> Chocolate dreamscapes ... Like cherry pie ... Make me weep ... Oh they make me cry! ... I wonder, I wonder ... What sort of blunder ... Makes the chances slim and painful ... That would be brought upon my life to cause me such situational turmoil!? ...

> Internal Resonance
Chocolate burns with vibrant colors...

o   In the middle of the night, I can hear them ... They call to me as if it were broad day light and I can see them for miles ... "Come hither into the light," they say to me as I cower in the cold clammy darkness ... While trying to find my shoes. Opening my eyes I see their faces closer now than ever before! ... They know me now ... It's no longer a dream like it once was! ... I speak to them with as much a voice as I can conjure at the time ... I speak to save my sanity from leaving me completely! ... I only get but a gesture of a word before I am cut off by the drums beating in the distance! ... Beating with such rhythm and course as to cause my own heart to beat with them! ... I look around and they are gone finally ... They have left me whole again ... This time! ...

> Perfectly Num ... B
Nom-nom-nom-nom-nom-nom-nom...

o   I have but one thing to say, so I will say it gently ... If you find it, she will come! ...

o   Orange makes me hungry, yellow makes me sad ... When I think of you, I am glad ... Sometimes I am happy, sometimes I am mad ... When I think of you ... It makes me want to kill your dad ... But only just a tad! ...

o   I look around and wonder where I am ... The clouds come down and wash away the phlegm ... I look up and down to see what I did ... Down smacks the hand as if I were a kid! ... I say to thee ... Oh I say to thee ... "Why does thou smackith me?" ...

o   If you were one of the merry men, then why do you cry? Why don't you die? ... It's easier, so much easier ... To ask me once again, twice is too much ... In the cabinet I keep my gun ... I look at you just for fun ... I call you to run ... I count to ten ... I count again ... And I look at your face as you contemplate your destiny ... Are you destine to die by the hand of your friend? If the answer is no ... Then you better start to run ... I will shoot you just for fun ... In the eyes of the elephant charged with my captivity ... I'm harmless as can be ... But don't trust me...

o   Inspiration comes from a can, you know you're the man, if you read the messages in your alphabet soup!...

➢ I'm Just A Normal Kind ... Of Guy *[Mood: Touched]*

o   Alas you poor ba*tards *[It's better than being r*tards]* ... Right? ... But what's the difference between re and bas? Aren't all tards created equal? Perhaps the difference is that ... Though everyone is born tarded, some have to be reborn ... While others are born without knowing who their fathers are! ... Maybe it's society's fault for coming up with such names and affixing them as they do!...

➢ So I was walking around one day and I came across this town ... So I calls my boy up and was like "Yo dog what you doing?" And he is like, "Nutin, wat you up to B?" Iz like, "Pick me up Bitch we gots to roll." So he sayz, "Where you at?" I come back and say, "I am in sane Bitch come get me!" ...

➢ For all you "Tots" out there, I'm the king of potato ... Mr. Head, eat your face out! ...

➢ 4 years on the force ... And I have come to realize ... That the diamonds in my eyes are shattered beyond repair ... The blood soaks through my hair; as I stare into your eyes ... As you circumcise ... My brain! ...

➤ Into the darkness comes from the light ... I met you and started my delight! ... Once there was an ounce of courage ... Said the poor boy alone! ...

➤ I walk in to the valley of the shadow of death and I look into my mind and realize ... There is a lot of room here, and I can totally fit my couch, loveseat, and 55" LCD TV ... There is no plasma here ... Now I just have to figure out how to get cable ... At least the rent is cheap! ...

➤ Sunshine On The Sidewalk

o Anger makes me happy, but I'm angry you are right ... I stand here in the corner, arguing to your delight ... I wait till you fall asleep, and stand over you all through the night ... I watch you lying there so soft and comforter-bound ... I wonder to myself as I wonder if I might ... As I watch you, I nary make a sound ... Slowly I think to myself as I creep closer still ... What if I do it, do I even have the will? ... As I pull the butter knife out from within my pants, my heart begins to dance ... Grabbing what thoughts I still have inside my head, I soon notice your body rustling within the bed ... I say a little riddle ... Softly within my mind ... Before I strike your eyes out, and make you go blind! ...

➤ Two Frogs On A Lily Pad

o Rigatoni, pasta formoni. I hate baloney. Or maybe that's bologna. I was once a man of the hour ... The man of great power I desired nothing but the best ... I cannot now understand what I meant by the rest of the story ... My features are all boring to me ... I am shoring to say the least! ... I understand the last bit of the plan at hand, but I cannot speak the truth of the plan to pass ... I make amends of the future to the past ... I cannot last to the thought of what is done ... I make the stories so short it seems sometimes I dream the end would come ... The time I sit and speak to myself in front of everyone ... Will soon pass into the darkness ... And followed will be the light that shimmers like gold reflecting from a shallow pond on a noon day sky on some distant wonderful land I cannot see! ... Unicorn tear drops, must be set free! ...

> I speak to you ... Not from the back of my mind ... But from the front of yours ... I see only what there is nothing to ... And speak of only what there is before me ... I cannot make this as I go. Day by day, as if I were in some dreamscape! I can only do as I am told by the beam. Such a miraculous sight it is to see one's own shadow within the light of unspeakable evil to which the light calls home. The shadows fear nothing of the cold clammy darkness he calls home ... For the night is surrounded by daybreak ... And it calms the innocents from within me to bring out the darkness I hide behind to keep me safe from what I cannot bring myself to see! ...

> I see you playing your trombone ... I see you sitting all alone ... I watch you as you take a breath ... And I see you as I see your death ... I watch you as you reach for the phone ... I watch you stand up calling home ... I see you and I stare into your eyes ... As I watch your slow demise ... You look right at me but you cannot see ... I know you see me ... But you cannot dream ... That I would be within your scream ... I always end up in a trance ... I always end up with a prance ... I like to watch you from a far ... I like to keep you in a jar ... I never sleep nor eat a meal ... I cannot feel! ... Have you guessed what I could be? That is right kids ... Just a humble tree! ...

[PAGE INTENTIONALLY LEFT BLANK]

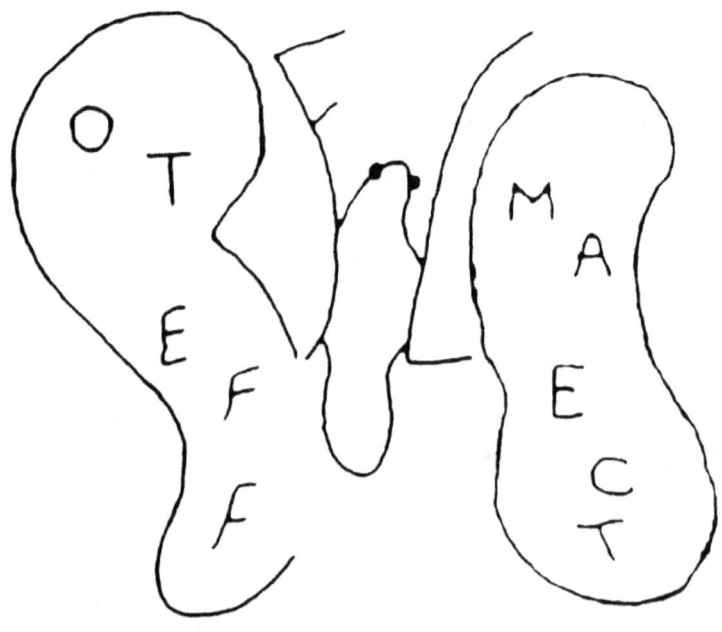

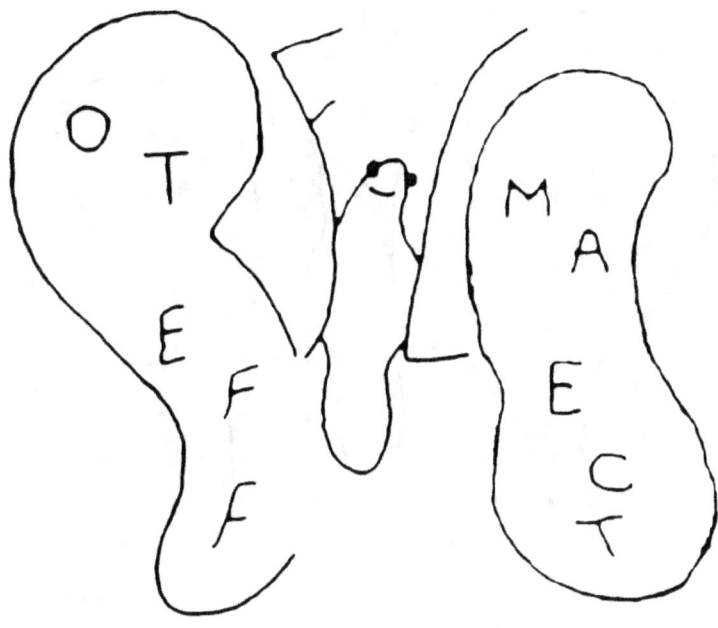

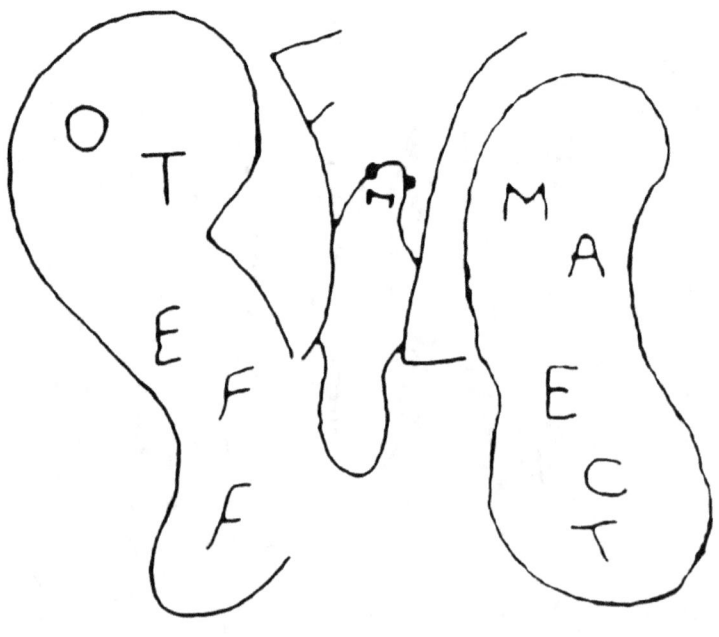

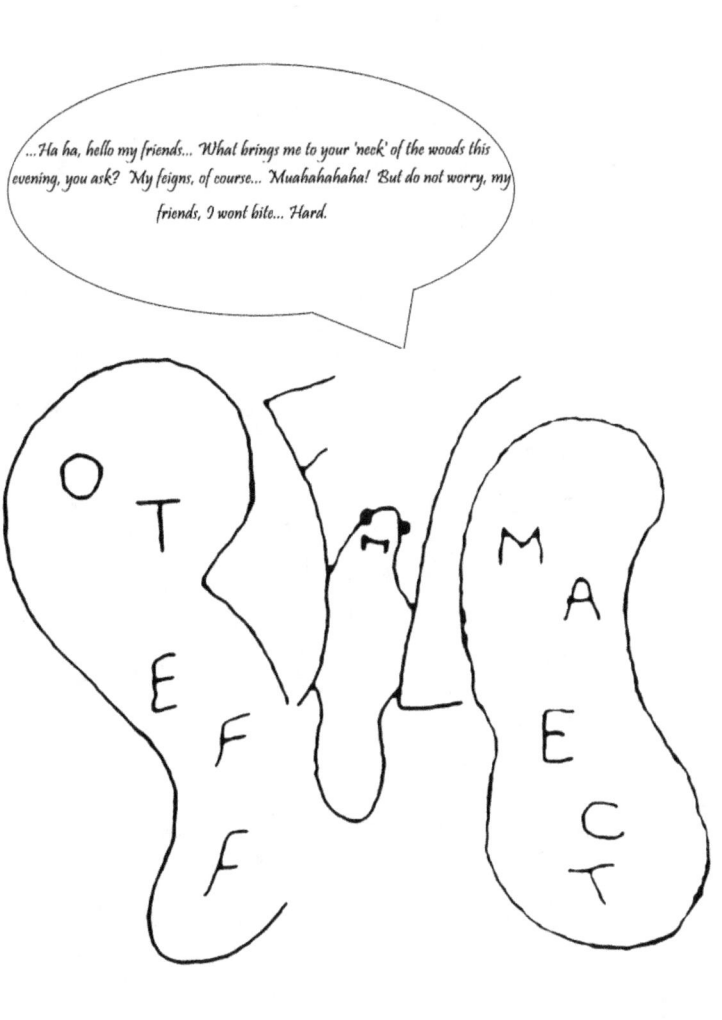

"Frog People Love Ceramics"

(-Rep. Tile Co., LLC)
(:6:)

➤ Orange Nation, Here I Come
    o   What time is it in here? What time is it
my dear? I want you to know that you're with me in my
ear. I hear you wanting more, and I can provide you to
score. I want to eat something to bore the time to shore
the roar in my car. I look inside of me, I cannot possibly,
understand what I see! It is me that I make to shake the
baking of the tree? As I look into your eyes, I wonder
what a surprise I could give you with the time it takes to
understand that I'm willing to choose to please you. Eat,
to ease you. I understand that you don't want to speak to
me. Should I kill you, should I spill all of your blood? I
can't see, I can't be, I can't eat, till I see you. I can't
breathe, I can't tease you. I have to know the truth, and I
look into your cold-dead eyes as I dig the hole to my surprise. I see you lying there without much care. I look at
you as I burn your hair. I wonder what you saw in me. I

wonder now as I start to see your brain fry in the fire so hot, I cannot stop, no I cannot! I look around and strain to see if anyone has spotted me. I cannot continue doing these things. As I start covering your bones with leaves, I run away and start a new life. I stare at your picture in my wallet as I tell you about my new wife. How good she is compared to you, how much I love her; oh yes, I do. You stare back at me with those cold-cold eyes, from deep in that picture you smile with demise. I watch you closely but not too close! I understand you hate me the most! I don't know what I did to anger, but I understand that you can't be mad at anyone but me for the time I took to buy you roses. When all you wanted was an ice cream Sunday. It was Saturday that day you died, I wonder now why didn't I cry. When I beat your head in with the mallet, or when I shoved your body in the ditch. I don't know, but it felt so good to me. I would have, if I could have, taken a pee. But I didn't want to disrespect you while I burned off your face. But before that, I washed it off with mace, just to make sure the fire would set right, and burn all through the night! ... Bottom line baby is ... I love you, even though you didn't take the name Mrs.! ...

> ➤ Look At Me As I Once Was, Then Again As I Am Now

  o I sit here as I look at the world and realize that I cannot control myself ... I wonder now as I wondered then ... Why do you call me 'friend'? I don't know you, and you don't know me ... But neighbor, will you not play that key? I look up, and then I look down ... And I pick up the knife left on the ground ... Some might say it was placed there ... But I cannot argue with the air ... I look around me and say to you ... "What are you gonna do?" I don't understand what you say back ... All I feel is the attack ... Quick to the draw, and fast to the field ... With this sword I now wield. Comes and goes, does the blood you feel ... From your head unto your heel. I cannot stop, not even now! Mr. Banana peel! ...

> Sparkle-sparkle Mr. Bang man ... Sparkle-sparkle with your bang hand ... Sparkle-sparkle Mr. Bang man ... Sparkle-sparkle no more as I can-can...

> Gingly, gangly, cut your head off as you sleep ... When I look into your eyes ... All I can see is death and demise ... When you look at me with your sad-sad face ... All I can see is a cold-cold place ... I cannot see myself with you ... I cannot see, or cannot do ... I cannot eat them while seated inside a lamb! ... I cannot ... will not ... Eat green eggs! ... No sir, ma'am! ...

> Read This ... It Will Change Your Life ... Or It Will Not ... Your call

o   In the palm of my hand I sit and ponder why I put myself here. I look into my eyes as I see the pain I have just caused ... Simply by standing up to you ... Deeply I wonder why I'm here ... And what there is for me inside those cold-cold eyes of yours ... Can you not hear my cries for help? ... My deepest desire to heal your pain goes but on false smiles and depth ears ... I sit back down and listen as you cry your pain away again ... Cry your pain away until you cannot cry anymore ... 'Till you fall asleep or worse ... As I sit there and watch you ... I think to myself, "Why?" A question of guilt and remorse for the pain and suffering I have nearly caused you ... And in turn caused myself ... I cannot even begin to understand why I have let the hurt I feel inside speak volumes upon my face to kiss the air and speak to you ... You cannot even fathom the unspeakable turmoil I am of witness to this day ... And every day I am left alive by what is inside of me ... I cannot let what I see ... And what beckons me to be free ... Free ... Until it is time for the coming of age that this day shall witness soon upon itself ... Into the night I shall contemplate the coming of the one that shall understand the true being of itself ...

And shall shed light upon what is the reality I see before me ... But not outside of what I cannot ... See which is within me ... The sky is turning red ... And all I see is wonderment around ... The sky is blue ... But around the blue is you ... And around you, is me ... So around me is the key ... The key of eternity ... I cannot contemplate the time it will take to be inside of you for so long ... You cannot understand the time it takes to man the guns and shoot the songs in two ... The son with my gun ... I shall be the one to do this for you! ...

➤ Porcupines Make Me Sad *[Mood: Cold]*

○ But I bet you didn't wonder where I hid the cash ... It was in the attic all the time ... As the world turns ... The world spins on me ... And as the world turns ... I feel just like a tree ... Planted with my outstretched arms to the few that follow me ... "Let it burn, let it burn ... Let it burn!" Says the gnome inside my head ... Let it burn to the ground and then soon they will all be dead ... *[Stop your singing now]*. I sit and ponder why I see these things I do ... And then I speak as if they were coming from you ... I raise my fist to hit them as I would ... But I shortly realize that does no good ... I sit here and study what I have done to hurt you ... And I sing this song ... But then, the gnome comes along ... The one that brings me flowers, and sings a jaunty song ... I wonder now, same as I did last year, and the time before my tears, and fear ... I cannot stop the staring of things ... I cannot hear your pleading, or rings ... The tone-deaf sound I scream in my ear ... Is one with such replace-able fear ... The only one that understands me is not ever here ... You speak to me and you say these things ... But I wonder why do you care about magic with wings? I don't even understand what you are about ... As I say this I hear you start to shout ... And I know that the end is never near! ... I understand this word that people call fear ... The populous is warning that too much exposure is deadly ... But what about too little is that not still severe? ... I look into my own eyes in the mirror ... And I understand you yet again, but this time not as much as before ... I know you know me, I know you care ... I know you know me, but how do you dare? ... I don't care ... I don't want to speak to you ... But how do you do it? ... How do you turn a blind eye to the pain you cause? ... Pain that suffocates life in general ... Pain that is so unspeakable ... Pain that has its own meaning to speak of ... And something to reek of? I call you here and I understand you never ... I don't even want to leave the lever ... What's wrong with you today? ... What can I call you, what can I say? You have to leave me alone in my own dismay! ... Perhaps I might even chance to say, I could become a display...

> Stealing Time Like A Fish In Heat

o Itsy bitsy vagabonds, tiny winy vaga-bonds. I once asked a man, I said, "How do you do?" And don't you figure, he said it back to you. Now a long time ago I walked down the street looking for something to eat ... And along came a spider ... Sat down beside her and stared at her curds and way ... She shrieked, and evaded ... Her place to stay ... And by the way ... Left her place behind ... In the time before the state was born ... And the time before was so hectic and more ... So I sat down to read! ... And along came a plea of the unfor-tunate few that duth breed to be ... Need to be ... And heed to be noticed ... I looked upon them and realized ... They needed me ... More than I knew at the time ... And by the rhyme ... I should have had them in the trap ... But oh crap ... It's sun down now ... And nary but a cow could escape the clutches of the simplest trap ... I set with my nap ... I looked into the woods ... And there in came the answer I was looking for all along ... An ending to my song ... I sat on a log ... And along came a frog ... But then the witness to the crime ... I squished what I will ... And then shot a pill ... Drank a glass of water till I ill. Because I can be the king ... When I wear my magic ring ... And when I die ... I die with pleasure! ...

➢ Psycho Robots In My Phace

o   I cannot see them ... Sam I am ... I cannot hear you claw my yam ... What will I be ... But spam to see ... What I see now ... I can Ma'am? ... Those that went that day are now in the far-far away ... Land that I cannot see ... Nor cannot be ... Nor cannot ... Will not be to be in the story...

➢ Disclaimer

o   Anything that you will read is only what I tend to bleed ... The postulations I know now ... Were only formulated by the cow! ... The misfit of the tainted one ... Shall be followed by the sun ... You look into my eyes so bright ... And then you see the distant light ... Follow it into the night ... And soon you shall be home my son! ... I look at you as you reach the door ... And soon you will be called on more ... The town is fighting for its gold ... And now you must be cast and sold! ... The story is as old as bread ... But it's not as costly as it is dead ... Into the mountains I have been ... And now I have just bumped my shin ... I ask for your forgiveness my friend ... For I will kill you in the end ... You only survive long enough to do ... What it is I want you too ... For I cannot end ... The nation without you! ... But once my story is told at last ... All I have to do is pass ... On to the next story I go! ... Lesson learned: Don't eat yellow snow! ...

➢ Life For Sale

Buy it quick, for it's going stale! ...

o   I sit here and watch the world go around me ... I sit here and watch the world stand still ... I sit here and watch the world go around me ... I sit here and start to feel ill ... The world plays tricks on my senses ... The world works in mysterious ways ... The world is filled with liars, jokers, and clowns with hilarious names ... I don't know how much longer I can go on like this without you in my life! ... I don't know how much longer I can go on like this without a reason to strife! ... The longer I look at the drawer ... The easier it is to pick up the knife ... And the longer I stare at the steel in my hands ... The easier it is to imagine the end of my plans ... The simplest of words make such progress even simpler ... The clock strikes one ... I reach for the gun ... The clock strikes two ... I load a bullet or few ... The clock strikes three ... That is game for me ... Bases are loaded and runners are tallied ... Two outs down, and the crowed is rallied ... One more inning is in the bottom and through ... Two more players ... And the game is a clue ... Stealing bases is like running races ... All you have to do is kill your opponent in the process ... Or make him lose his popularity and poise! ... That should crack him up to make some noise! ... Then you can use the verbiage he speaks of you to write him down and clown around ... Before you have to run the poles ... 98% chance of error ... No one is looking ... So vote for Binky, the high wire clown ... He should win ... For he'll never let you down ... With a smile or two ... Binky is the clown of the hour ... But did you know he used to be a mime? ... But is that really a crime? ... Switching sides ... Or ... Allegiance to state of a dress? ... One should think not ... But mimes can only be trusted for some time ... Because only true clowns know how to turn a frown into a smile! ... And we haven't been talking about the upside-down variety in a while! ...

> Cross Roads

o   In this time in my life I'm left with choices I can't decide ... Do I stick with the path I'm on? Do I venture into the unknown? ... Should I keep traveling down this beaten path? ... Or should I go back home? I wonder why I keep on traveling ... And I wonder why I am still here ... In the middle of the evening I look unto the clock ... Half past five it says ... But nary smidgen of walk ... The time it takes for me to snooze ... And half cock the button back ... Is the same time it would take to replace the batteries in the clock ... Sitting here, I ask my mind to just refrain ... Stop these thoughts you think all day ... Just put down and step away ... Do you not know you are hurting me ... Deep within my brain you see? You cannot know the troubles I have ... You cannot know nor will not at all! ... I read these things on the bathroom wall ... And sure enough I will just call ... To get the time ... And perhaps some noise ... Back to back ... I hear them boys ... Into the alter the call is made ... Someone orders triple chocolate and a glass of lemonade ... I ask the pastor, "What's in the punch?" He whispers, "Shh," and, "There's not much! ... Just a drop or more of a pour ... A little sider with much-much more!" ... You call this a friendly game ... In the name ... Oh I will be tame! ... Do not think too clearly ... For this is only a test ... Now place your fist at ease and rest! ... Breathe in and out but do not shout! ... For they can hear your screams of distress ... I must regress ... You cannot fight me ... You cannot win! ... But if I lose you ... I have your twin ... One of us is gonna die! ... And I will just turn into a fly ... In the middle of the day ... You will fly away and stay ... But if you choose to be the star ... Please just get up out your car ... Run away and run real fast ... For you just ran yourself out of gas ... The closest place is five miles away ... You might just get there in time for day! ...

➢ Cannot right, or even reason with meter ... What should I do Stan? ... Should I eat her? ... Stan calls me back and answers my questions with a question. ... "Do you like sea food or Chinese?" ... I ponder that and tell him "Yes!" But realizing this is a test ... A trick-question at best ... Because both answers lead me to the same thing in the end ... A feeling of satisfaction within a friend ... In-you-end-oh's are best between friends I guess ... So come on baby, just wear a dress, or a skirt ... It does the same job ... I won't act like a slob if you bob on my knob ... Can you get my reason for pleasing you like I can? ... Or can I? Um, help me out here Stan! ... Into the night, I call the kite ... Play with me to play my plight! ... And the wind that beckons thee ... Shall also beckon me! ... Fortunes are won and lost on the interstate ... And at that rate ... They are closing fast ... But I just past ... My exit ... At last, I cannot wait 'till my date ... The court hath granted me the simple privilege to see ... The Muh-pets, on frozen water, in 3D...

> Intro To Chaos ... In Yo Phace!

o   Excuse me as I literarily mind-**** you in the *** ... But please ... Oh please ... Pass the bees ... Oh they are just cruising by ... And when I see that twinkle in your eye ... I just want to stab it out and place it on some toast with jam ... Oh and ma'am, could you pass the coffee? ... I see Juniper trees on the horizon as I pass the interstate ... And contemplate what I have done for starts here ... What are you gonna do my deer? ... You look deeply into my eyes ... As I pass out from boredom and beer ... I call you to the table in my house ... And I speak softly so as not to stir the mouse! ... One day I shall be in the kingdom of the forest ... And one day I will roam ... You call me when I am at home ... And I answer not as myself ... As I put my feelings in the jar on the shelf ... I say some words you want to hear, I say "I love you," and I call you my dear ... Then somehow the phone disappears ... Only to come back but you are not here ... I call you back but there is no answer ... As if you ponder ... I pause and strife ... The kitchen was where I felt safe before! ... So I go there but nevermore ... I am done with this ... And done with that ... All I see is the Che-shire Cat ... He looks at me with his unwinking smile, I stop him now … Or for a while! … I cannot look into his eyes … For up top his head is his disguise … One time I sat here looking at the way I look at me … The wall was there when I took a pee … You stare into my eyes so long … That I forget you are always wrong! … I call your name in great despair … And wonder if you will be there … To heed my warning … And respond to my call … For am I only talking to the wall? … Or is it me that is even real at all? …

> Cut Me

○   I should want you to know, I just feel like going slow … I hate you now! … I know you do … You have me here … But you hate me too! … "One of you will kill me soon!" Jezus said as he reached for his spoon … The Angry hatter once said "Drink up fast or lose your ass!" So again I said it … And again I have shown … You know me more than you have felt me hone my bone … You know me like you say you do … But you could not hold up to the power of glue … I call your name in the wind sometimes … Just so I can hear it whistle through the chimes! …

> Pitter Pater Of

○   … Little feet? No-no, that's "Just the meat" … Dropping on the ground, said the clown trying to prepare a steak for lunch … Just wipe it clean and slap it with a punch … Tender meat is much more sweet … With some sticky nature to marinate … And as we sat atop the hill … Overlooking the people we would soon kill … We made a pack that night … That no one would escape into the light … I look back now, and wonder why … Why did I not shoot into the sky? The dawn was bright and big as a whale, but sooner now there shall be the tale … For once in a while I call out to thee … Make your amends only to me! … For once I forgive you … You shall be free … And never again will you need to beckon me to save thee … Into the summer winds … The walrus calls ... And then does the softness of the east wind remember ... That when there is light there is danger ... Only shadows fear the dark ... But one might recall that no one would ever see the evil within that allows me to be ... One day I shall make your name my name ... And then I shall tame the wild lions of the east river ... Running through this town and that! ... They terrorize the village to speak the language of the spoken few ... I only wonder what it would be like to be in the path of destruction ... So I can learn a few things about your life! ... You ask me one thing after another and I tell you that the answer never has changed! ... But you keep asking me ... And asking me ... To the point I tell you something different just to see your reaction ... But it doesn't seem to matter to you anymore! ...

➢ What?

○ Tom, your sight is the bomb ... But I must regress ... Is this just a test? ... I might be in my own extended network ... But I can't have myself as a friend? ... What will be the end? ... If I were to own myself as a game ... I could not play with myself even if I were tame? ... You know me ... As I look around I see ... What I can't see without knowing that you're really me ... Inside you look around and you find what I hide ... These feelings that burn me like a light shown through a hole ... Deep within my very soul! ... But I don't believe in such talk as much as I believe in the mock ... So when I was back in the day ... The days of wood-stalk ... Again ... And again ... And again ... They play with the band ... And now I know the true meaning of sand ... The stuff that fills my ears ... Tears ... And years growing up ... But life was better when I was a pup! ... You never know what you will be ... Until you take a long look at what you were ... Are ... And are gonna see! ... You have to look into the mirror once or twice to get the picture just right ... Before you go out and mess up your night! ... You count to ten ... And then again you count backward ... Just to know you're number one in your heart ... Even if everyone else knows you're just an old fart! ... No style or rhythm to speak of ... Not even a sense of functionality to leak ... Or even reek of! ... I smell the stench of defeat ... But let's pass that shop by ... And go get something to eat! ... I'm hungry and my stomach is sore ... For I haven't eaten in a week or more! ...

➤ I Am A

o   ... Cereal killer ... Every morning I wake up ... The captain stares me down ... And like a clown I follow in suit ... "You want to give me the boot!?" He says as I pass by the cabinet door ... As if he is calling out for more ... It should be labeled as abuse ... For the way that I constantly am in use! ... I call to you from up-top the floor ... But you only read my lips as if I am asking for more! ...

➤ One Plus One Makes Three

o   Do the math and I'll tell you what to do ... One day I will call to you ... And you will respond to me ... "Please, just oh please will you not be ... My neighbor?" Of course you will, or I will kill ... The clock on the wall ... So you will stay the night with not a sight of land ... You say my name with biter-sweetness on your breath ... Like you just got finished finishing off the stay-puffed marshmallow man... *[He always stays puffed]*. Into the night I look into my soul ... And into the light I look into the hole ... Look at me with Spanish eyes ... Then give them back to her while you finish putting on your disguise! ... But the real test is just the best ... You have to find me Waldo ... And when you do ... Punch that sorry sob in the balls ... And tell him that I spent the better half of a decade looking for his punk ass in the beach scene ... And all I found was a funky striped hat and a sign that read ... "Be back in 5 min, Sincerely, Waldo." ... But he never showed! ...

➤ Retarded ... But Don't You Have To Be Tarded First?

o   In the field ... Of my mind ... I find myself ... Behind ... And when I look ... Into your eyes ... I can see ... My demise! ... As I look ... Into your soul ... All I can see ... Is the mole! ... The one who chases my dreams away ... As soon as I start to play ... When you call out my name ... I feel all the joys in this game! ... You look at me ... But then look away ... And now all I'm left with ... Is myself to play ... The number one time that you feel alone! ... Why don't you just give this dog a bone? ... You know me ... And I know you ... You tell me what you want me to do ... Make me hurt! ... You make me cry! ... Make me wonder ... Why oh why? ... But do not make me hurt a fly! ... Until you say my name again ... Until you call me out my friend ... Until you bleed like me in the end! ... I say sorry once or twice ... I say sorry in a vice ... But sorry does not cut the cheese! ... It Only relieves ... Until you say please! ...

➤ Juniper Skies

o   If you look at the world today ... You might speak to say ... A little song or two should fill your heart ... And blind your soul! ... Look at me ... I'm on a roll! ... One by one ... And two by two ... I look at myself ... As I also look at you ... You say these things ... And then you speak to me ... As if to drink ... I sit on a corner and ponder my life ... I look around and start to strife! ... The bums watch closely ... And peer far and wide ... They look at me with doubt ... For there is nowhere left to hide! ... As I come across the subway entrance ... I look upon the floor ... I see them at the door ... And they are calling me for more! ... I stop aside the railway ... And I look up and down the track ... Something touches my back ... And I fall upon the floor ... I scream out for the world to stop ... This pain it causes me! ... But by now you witness ... The troubles that I see! ... I'm hurt deep inside my soul ... Since you are without me! ...

> ➤ Would You Be My
>> o   ... Neighbor? Could you be my? ... Should you be my? ... I don't know why I even ask why! ... You only want me for what you can't have ... And you know I want the same! ... But alas I can't be one of those guys ... Those perfect models of perfectuousness! ... Due to the little fact that I'm not on the scene as much ... Nor do I pack that sort of punch! ... You look at me ... And you know the truth! ... I look at you as I step up to the booth ... I pay my time ... And as if it were a crime ... I get knocked right into the back of the line! ... I said it once ... And twice again ... You might as well stay as my friend! ... You know you want to ... And I know you too ... You just need to get a clue! ... I write this not to be so un-content ... But just as a way to unre-lent ... I look around the room ... And I see myself ... I cannot see right past the shelf ... You look around the room ... Perhaps you see the wicker broom ... I left it there ... To throw you off my scent! ... But I must re-pent! ... I have sinned again ... And again ... But that is not why I call to him! ... You understand my plan at hand ... But you don't like to realize! ... That these other guys ... Cannot stand me ... Cannot stand to have me around ... Nor have me clown them down! ... I know how much better I am then them! ... And not to be cocky ... But well ... So is my jockey! ... In the middle of the time ... I asked myself why? ... I said, "Hello sir ... Can I help you?" ... And me being the self I am ... I said, "Yes ... Yes you can too." ... So as I was talking to myself ... In the alleyway ... I pondered one little question ... And one question alone ... Why oh why ... Would you give a dog

a bone? … Then it hit me … To give a dog a home! … And then to let him roam … So someone else can give a dog a bone … The cycle of life … To have a fish is to eat for a day … But to learn to fish … Is to be aggravated in every special way! … I have angst and the common cold … Or so the doctor tells me … I would rather listen to my bread mold … At least it can get me well! … And it's not quite as old! … But you never know … What that could bring … Perhaps one day … I might even have my own ring … One that chimes my name … And even feels quite tame! … But with a bite of sorts … Enough of a kick … To knock you out of your shorts! … But only for those … Who are being good sports! …

- ➢ Ninjas
  - o N - Stands for Ninjas…
  - o I - Stands for the I in Ninjas … I also like ninjas…
  - o N - Is the second N in Ninjas … It is similar to the first N in Ninjas … It does look similar, but upon closer examining … You will notice that it is second, because it is lazy … Or its alarm fails to go off on time … Unless it's the first N in Ninjas' sibling … And they switch places every once in a while, then you are on your own, kid! … Unless it's the first N in Ninjas in disguise … Like a true ninja could be! …
  - o J - Clearly is involved in Ninjas…
  - o A, I am talking about Ninjas … So keep it down! *[Frowny face]* Don't make me sick my ninjas after you…
  - o S - Allows for one Ninja to become many in the blink of an eye … Almost as fast as rabbits … Almost … Which makes one wonder if rabbits aren't just ninjas in disguise … Perhaps they are! …
- ➢ Aggravation *[Mood: Crushed]*
  - o You know when you think everything is honestly how it is said to be … But you are told afterward

that it's really not that way? ... And what you were told was just a lie? ... Like you have been played for the fool ... And when you try to get things strait ... And to the point that you're shot out of the conversation ... Or completely cut off by either external sources ... Or otherwise ... Yeah, Rubik's cubes are hard for me too! ...

➤ The Penguin Flies At Midnight

○　"Follow me on a journey of your dreams!" ... A woman off in the distance screams ... You sit here joking ... But hear such noise ... You often play ...Without your toys! ... I call to you on a summers eve ... And you look at me ... And call me Steve ... You watch me closely ... As I pass by ... The night is young ... And you're about to die! ... I hold your lifeless body close ... And almost chance to see your ghost ... I nary speak ... But much to quiver ... And you're still standing to deliver ... Notice fast ... As you were waiting on me to pass ... To take the bullet of your mind! ... I should have told you ... To stand behind! ... The walls were thick enough ... To cushion the blow! ... But I knew ... It would not take too much longer ... Before the truth ... Would be told ... So set the mood ... And open the book ... One must not chance to spoil the look! ... I look upon your face ... But one last time ... And then I start to hum a rhyme ... A tiny melody to calm my nerves! ... But all I can think of are the verbs! ... Ones that encounter the night on this chilly eve ... The ones that accompany my name of "Steve" ... You said those words so easily to me ... And I made the faces you often wanted to see! ... The history between us two ... Was often held together with glue ... But nevertheless ... I stand my ground and keep to my paces ... The horse I bet on ... Won only two races! ... I lost the bet all up in the end! ... But at least this time I brought me a friend! ... Cold of iron ... I smell in the air ... Careful now there comes many a stare! ... Faster now is my pace of pulse ... The story must be told as false ... Save my sanity ... I must try to do! ... For if I were to say ... The wrong shoes were on you! ...

➤ I be righting, you be reading ... I be "Yo hey," you be "There they!" ... There they, be there ... There you, be square ... No one, has hair! ... Unless, they there ... One, two, three, for ... You won this door! ... No one, has hair, except them there! ... They all, have one ... Piece chocolate, yum, fun! ... Can you read me? Story, grape tree! ...

➤ Look man ... I can't take it! ... I have searched everywhere ... But I can't find it! ... They told me it was there ... They told me it was easy to find! ... But what they didn't tell me ... Was that it was even easier to leave behind! ... You have to help me ... You have to know ... In the dead of night ... Limes do not glow! ... They also ... Prefer sunlight, to snow! ...

➤ You knew me, and you let me go ... Why did you let me go? ... Why, why did you let me go? ... For shame ... For shame! ... For shamus! ... One o'clock, two o'clock, 3 o'clock, Bok-Bok-Bok ... Wrap a weasel in a cloth! ... Rap the weasel ... Tap the weasel ... And take my easel, Bok-Bok-Bok ... I watch the hands ... As they count down ... *[Blank]*-turn the corners ... Of my frown! ... Like my eggs ... Sunny-side ... Up! ... As I sit down! ... Painfully happy ... Just like a pup ... But unlike the clown! ...

➤ You can't fight what you can't see ... Unless you're blind! ... Oh, forgive me ... But you better be a ninja ... With a black belt of at least 3! ... Or else you will not stand a chance ... Against my French fry tree! ...

➤ You can't stop ze running, de will not cause ju to make yur appointamente past due, mon frendio! ... Das cluck ticker tocks mine ears hoff ... I ere ju das burst thyme, don't mirror yur words ... Juan cun only take so mutch ... Me drive der, ju self, I will ... Red you get, now...

➢ If I rehearse this free verse for too long, it will make things worse between us ... I will head back to Mars ... You head back to Venus! ... Upon my return back to this place where we have stagnated our relationship ... Here's a tip ... It wasn't all my fault! ... Perhaps that is a separate lesson you should place into your mind vault! ... Because I'm done chipping away ... Only to realize I should have left ... Yesterday! ...

➢ All I can see is what is within ... Pull back the skin ... And let's begin ... You dive right in ... But back stroke the shin ... Two days ago ... We were kin ... I back-pack through ... You're ruptured as I will ever be ... That this is the way to go ... Said the guide ... But little did he know ... That we have been circling the same spot for days ... But I'll keep feeding him lies ... Till he tells us the truth! ...

➢ You turn pages like the clock turns time ... Reading every single rhyme ... You sit back into your comfy chair ... And you pretend that I'm not there ... I pass you, but it's all the same! ... It's ok, I'll take all the blame! ... Even though none of this was ever my fault! ... But this time ... I'll seal my heart inside a vault ... And only I will retain the key ... So to get at my heart ... You'll have to go through me! ...

➢ Taking off my skates ... I look at the clock ... It's getting late ... I realize I have no time ... I must finish you off ... And then grab a lime ... You plead with me to let you be ... "I cannot!" ... I say ... No time ... Waste away ... So off now ... Into the sunset I go ... Another time ... But no one will know! ...

➢ Toxicity is a mystery ... Simplistically ... I'm just too real you see! ... But you can't see ... Except in 3D! ... With classes B ... But I gots 20 ... 20-20 vision ... But I aint fishin' ... For no lines ... I gots all I needs ... But I'll mirror up ... So I have double vision! ...

➢ I steal time … I steal righteousness … I steal rhymes … I steal lichens' fists! … You steal from me … You steal all you can! … But you can't steal my heart … For I am a tin man! …

Prunes: They're Not Just Good To Eat

("They Also Drive Slow On The Freeway")
(:7:)

NEUTRALLOGUE (*ÆTE*)

"... And Jill came tumbling after, the end ... I hope you have enjoyed this rendition of the stunning tale of *Jack and Jill*, during their arduous trip up a hill. Only to have it end in peril and tragedy. So tune in next week for another epic tale of suspense, betrayal, and murder ... For we will be reading *Hey Diddle-Diddle, The Cat And The Fiddle* ... Good night boys and girls." The curtains drop and the lights go dim ... *Mistery-Pieces Theater* ends. The host gets out of his comfy chair, takes off his robe and ascot, and leaves for coffee.

Dressed only in his under garments, he comes back and realizes the room is quite frigid, and just down right cold. Looking around, he notices there is someone inside the room with a mop and a broom. "Hello, how are you?" He calls out. "I'm ok," says the man, "Just cleaning up the place a little ... I'm the janitor, how are you sir?" "I'm doing just fine ... This room seems a bit cold to me at the moment though." The host forgot that during his tapings, the room's air conditioner setting is lowered so he can wear his highly insulated robe with a fire in the background, to set the mood of the program. But between tapings they shut off the fire to conserve gas, though they keep the air conditioner setting the same. As the host and janitor converse, the host sizes up the janitor presently cleaning the otherwise vacant room. The janitor turns around to wring out his mop and start on a different place in the room, when all of a sudden, the host moves into position behind the janitor. Without warning the host grabs a pipe off the floor, and knocks the janitor unconscious.

Pulling a knife from his sock, the host uses it to slice the janitor's neck, and down the center of the janitor's body making a "T". Then, the host scoops out the inner parts of the janitor, making sure to preserve as much of the skin as possible.

The host then makes sure he got everything out of the janitor's skin that he wanted before picking up the mop and cleaning up after himself. After cleaning up the blood, and other stains on the floor from the mess he made, the host brings the now gutted and hollowed out skin of the former janitor to his secretary to take to the dry cleaners; and have it pressed for the following week's show. The host then goes home...

The following week, the host returns to work to the relief of himself; he notices a cellophane incased "man-suit" that is the late janitor's skin. Like a little kid, the host is thrilled to have such a turnaround; he rips open the packaging to his man-suit, to which he begins trying it on for a proper fit. "They even added a zipper and buttons!" He giddily exclaims to his secretary *[Excited happy face]*

as he sports an erection which, causes the man-suit to also be erect.

His secretary turns her head away as she mentions to
the host that he may want to do something about his little
problem that seems to be growing, "Gladys, whatever do
you mean?!?" He says to her as he looks down, "Ah,
well, I just really enjoy this suit, and tonight I will definitely be the man of the hour as I bed many a chick while
going clubbing dressed in my super-fly suit!"

Like a coverall-hoody hybrid, the new "man-suit" is
on the host. But, no sooner does he get his suit fitted just
right, when, it's show time. So, with no time to readjust
and get rid of his erection, or even take off the suit; the
host makes his way to the comfy chair as is. He puts on
his robe and ascot, over his man-suit, and arranges in
front of him the big book of nursery rhymes, to cover his
erection, as he begins his normal routine of telling stories
to children ... "Good evening boys and girls, and welcome to tonight's reading of *Hey Diddle-Diddle, The Cat
And The Fiddle*, A story of ... Click."

WINTERLOGUE (*NINE*)

"Ducky, have you seen my shoes?" Calling from the
back room this morning, I ask Ducky if he had seen my
shoes, I have misplaced them. *[Sad face]* "I have not,"
He yells back before heading into the living room so as to
prepare for his day. "I found them. *[Happy face]* They
were under the bed again this morning." I turn off the
TV and head to the kitchen to begin making breakfast,
the second, esq. *[duce]* for the both of us before we head
to our respective works today.

We finished breakfast and I drove Ducky to his job at
Miko's Sacred Garden, before heading to run some er-
rands, then heading off to my own job. I couldn't help
but think of that girl from last night though, and I had a
feeling that Ducky was also thinking of his girl too. I
looked over at him as I drove down the road, but I

couldn't really tell what was going on inside his head. He caught on that I was staring at him but he remained inanimately still, and just looked ahead at the road as if to gesture for me to watch where I was driving.

I took the hint and focused on the road. We finally arrived at work and I mentioned to Ducky, to have a good day; I would be back to pick him up after work. He nodded and walked inside the building as I drove off down the street.

SPRINGLOGUE (*BOUNCY*)

"So there I was, on the road again, all alone in this dusty land ... Yes there I was, all alone again, nowhere left to hatch a plan ... No one ever gonna come around, no one ever gonna put me in the reigns again! No one left to clown me down ... I just have to say, I just miss the way ... I miss the way you always let me down! ..."

I have no idea what that guy is always singing about, or why I always put his record on while I drive to work. Hmm, sometimes I just don't see why I do a lot of the things I do. But no matter, I'm here at work; am I parked right? *[Gets out and checks parking]* Yeah, I'm fine. Where was I? Right, off to my job; heh, time to make the donut holes! Ha-ha-ha-ha-ha, oh yeah!

[Raised eyebrows, smiley face]

[Out of nowhere something flashes in the sky]

"What was that?" I wondered to myself out-loud. Out of the corner of my eye, there was a girl standing out of the corner of that building. I walked right up to her and asked if she had seen the same thing I did. "I haven't the slightest idea as to what you're talking about." She replied, "What 'thing' are you referring to? For I see many 'things,' all or none of which could be the vary one you bespeak of!" I sat there, standing, for a little bit trying to gather the words like a school child gathers poesy's; but I was at a loss. I finally spoke with the words I could find, and told this young girl that she only need close her eyes to see what I might have saw.

Within the golden fruit there is a shiny apple. Open your hand and see the raisin residing there grow into a tiny raisin man, and watch as he bands together with his friends to form a signing group that will forever change the world; until they are forgotten and fade away into obscurity like those before them; and like those after them will follow.

You're seated in a chair, in your hand there is a ball. In your other hand there is a box, the box has a top that is open. Inside the box is a worm, the worm has glasses, because he is near sighted and they are prescription. He doesn't like them, but his mother insists he wears them so that he can read and write more effectively; although they makes him not eligible to play sports at his school, he does as his mother suggests and wears them; despite his other interests. The worm stands up, opens the door in the box and walks onto your hand, he waves a hello to you as we walks up your arm and onto your shoulder.

Once at your shoulder, the worm looks at the ball in your other hand, the one not involving the box. He makes a notion that he wants to dive onto the ball. You look at him and motion your head like that's a bad idea, he shakes his head in protest to your protest and tells you to watch his glasses as he takes them off his face; his mother would be quite disappointed in him if he lost them, or broke them. You finally say ok to the worm and agree to keep his glasses safe from harm. He places them on your shoulder and takes a leap toward the ball. As you watch him dive toward this ball in your hand, you can't help but notice his incredible form and posture, "His technique is flawless!" You utter as you watch his descent; and you begin to wonder if he has ever practiced before, or if this is all just natural talent. The worm nears the ball on his decent from your shoulder and you start you get anxious, you start to cringe; you start to worry if the tiny worm will hurt himself when he contacts the hard surface of the ball in your hand, or will something save him, "Will nothing be done that could stop this daredevil worm from being nothing more than a cruel joke of reality, or a mere pawn of purpose?" But then you notice, ahead of the worm's path, in the palm of your very hand itself, there is not a ball at all, there is in fact a miniature Olympic pool where the ball once stood, and into it, the worm completes his dive; as all the audience and judges applaud his performance and award him 10's all around.

You begin clapping too; as you are caught up in this momentous occasion of such, that a worm could gain a perfect dive score, nay that! That any diver could gain such perfect dive scores from such judges as are witnesses this day. These are of the toughest judges alive, and they demand perfect performance; or no performance at all! After the crowd dies down, you get up from the stands and walk up to the worm and congratulate him on his performance, and ask him what he will do next? He looks at you quite inquisitively and mentions that he has never been to the moon. You ponder back at him and mention that you have never been there either. He leans over and whispers into your ear, "Would you like to go there with me?" You feel a bit of excitement stirring as you whisper back, "Yes!!!"

A Wall erupts from the floor and secludes you within your own room, you're changed in both clothes and skin tone; now outside you notice a shiny coin is shaking his head at you, and you yearn to pick it up. Opening the door you see a jungle outside growing all the more junglier; but you venture outside so you may ascertain the whereabouts of the coin you seek. A jaguar whispers for you to follow it, but you seem to think his emissions are too far below standards for your ears. But what is that you see off in the distance? A puma comes running quickly from the north, he brings word of a generation lost to the seasons, but he is having a hard time telling his tale to you, you finally tell him to just do it already and it will be over before another brand of animal catches your attention this day, then it's too late!

Just like those crackers down the street, they think that just because they live in a shiny red box, with a giant string on the roof, that they can bring down our property value by placing all their discarded, disfigured, body parts all over the place. It's bad enough that some of them are born without heads or faces, and some are ass-less, why even the asses have no asses!

"Bo-trickle-tickles, Bo-trickle-trickles, Bo-trickle-trickles, Bo-trickle-trickles, wha-wha ... Bo-tickle-trickles, Bo-trickle-trickles, Bo-trickle-trickles, Bo-trickle-trickles, wha-wha ... Bo-trickle-trickles, Bo-tickle-trickles, Bo-trickle-trickles, Bo-trickle-trickles ... Ba-ba-bo, ba-ba-bo, ba-ba-bo, ba-ba-bo, trickle-trickle-trickles ... Wa-wa..."

Banana, Banana Banana, Banana, Banana, Banana, Banana, Banana, Banana, Banana, Banana, Banana, Banana, Banana, Banana, Orange.

What did the orange say to the banana? Nothing, but she did get away and called the cops, the banana was later charged with grape. *[It is a serious offense; frowny faces all around]*

SUMMERLOGUE (*SAUSAGE*)

"Open your eyes." Jill, my coworker, said; "Surprise, we got you a cake for your birthday, and decided to surprise you today!" "You guys," I said. With glee in my voice and a surprised look on my face as all my friends and coworkers were gathered around my desk. "You're always messing with me ... Thank you!" I blew out the candles on the tiny cupcake in front of me and listened to them all wish me happy birthday; followed by pleasantries and chit-chat before we all returned to work.

There was a knock on my door a little bit later in the day, and I looked out the window right at that moment to notice a small bird fly by and poop on my car parked on the side of the road. I could have sworn I just washed that car earlier in the day, and now it's ruined. But I guess that's what you get when you don't pay to park in the garage like everyone else, and you simply decide that the "Free parking" is just too good of an idea to pass up, especially when you're running late.

"Hey, Dreamy Mcdream-Dream, wake up, your shift is in two-minutes and you have people to sit." Are the words that startle me from my nap I've found myself in while waiting in the break room for my shift at work to start "Yes Mr. Popanuchi, I'm on it right now," getting up from my seat, I head to the front of the restaurant and with a smile on my face; and a heart heavier than gold, I walk two hungry guests to their seats and hope they like where I have seated them. Then I head back to my post as the most glorious of head host, but I try not to boast!

The time passes as does the mountain of masses, the clock on the wall keeps me in line, but all I can think of is the taste of that wine, when my thirst will be quenched will involve the number nine.

Another day down, and another dollar made, I gots bills, and other such expenditures, so I gots to get paid! But finally it does, as will every day; the clock strikes my name, and so goodbye I must say. To my coworkers, and my job, that guy on the corner, I think his name is Bob. "Fare thee well to you all and to you all a good night; I hope all of you are well, and that the bugs in your bed do not bite!"

Arriving, at the bus stop, I notice that there is a cop, he looks in my direction, and has to hide his erection, at the site my donuts; I mention softly that these are just holes. Just then he turns on his siren, and sooner then I realize, he confiscates my holes; all of them. *[Frowny face]*

FALLLOGUE (*HOTT*)

After work, I run by where Ducky works to pick him up. "Miko, is Ducky still in the kitchen?" I ask, "No, he left thirty-min ago," Said Miko. I had a fowl feeling about that statement, but I decided to venture on anyway and look at the usual places my fine-feathered friend liked to waddle off to after work. After searching for around two hours, I couldn't find him anywhere! I decided to stop by *Miko's Sacred Garden* again to see if he might have still been at work and Miko just didn't realize he was there.

I got to the restaurant, and noticed there was an extra duck hanging in the window that I hadn't noticed on my last trip earlier in the day. It seemed quite freshly de-feathered, and hung. I was curious too because he seemed so familiar to me as well. I asked Miko about the new bird, because something smelled fishy, and that was odd because they don't serve fish in this restaurant. Miko assured me that the duck in question was prepared by Ducky himself earlier in the day; but they didn't put him out until a little bit ago since they were so backed up on other duties for the restaurant. I was slightly relieved, but I was still curious as to where Ducky might have gone. Miko gave me no help, all she said was that Ducky left and might have headed south. Such a stereotypical thing to say, I thought, but I left and went home all the same. "Perhaps he is already home." I mentioned out-loud before I left. "Yes, perhaps he is!" Miko said, agreeably, too agreeably I thought! But I shook off the notion and headed out the door to my car anyway.

I arrived home, and the place was empty. Not a sign of life was hung in the air *[The poster people gave me a choice of posters when I bought the t-shirt, and I chose that one; even though Ducky didn't like it, and even tore it down each time I would put it on the wall, so I was relieved that no one had messed with it. But that began to worry me].* I looked around and saw an empty beer can on the floor, I knew it wasn't mine, since I usually recycle my aluminums; and I also separate my trash for easy recycling too, but It was also not the brand of beer Ducky usually drinks. "Ducky, are you here?" I called out, but there was only silence; an eerie silence that I just couldn't really shake.

"D-Ducky? ... A-are y-you t-there? ... Ducky!?" Again, there was only silence that replied. I was starting to wonder what might have happened to Ducky. As I wondered, I started to worry, I start to get anxious and I started to feel like maybe Miko was not being forthcoming with me earlier when she mentioned that Ducky had left work. Maybe she meant that Ducky had "checked out", but that he had not quite left the premises. I started thinking more about how Miko would look at Ducky; at first I thought it was just infatuation for my friend, but as I began to think more about it, I have noticed that there were often times that I could see Miko de-feathering Ducky with her eyes as he walked back into the kitchen on a few occasions that I would stay a little longer when dropping him off at work, before going about my normal routine.

"I just don't understand it; Ducky is bound to be somewhere, isn't he?" I asked aloud, hoping that someone might answer my thoughts. But alas, only silence again was the greeting party to my worries. "I know what I'll do." Said my outside voice, as a thought of calling the neighbors to *Miko's Sacred Garden* and asking if they saw Ducky leave work, and if they knew where he might have gone. "Hello, can I speak to Mr. Smith please?" I said to the woman who answered the phone. "Please hold, he is with someone right now," She replied.

"This is Mr. Smith, how can I help you?" Said he, "Yes, I'm wondering if you noticed whether a mellow yellow fellow left the Chinese-food restaurant next to your establishment earlier this evening?" I asked him. "No, I can't say that I did, I've been quite busy with my own customers and other business ventures; but as I understand it, no one fitting that description left the restaurant today." He retorted. "I see, well thank you for your time." I said as I hung up the phone. There I was, left with no leads and no one to turn to except for Miko and her word as to the fact that Ducky left unharmed after his shift was over. But today there seemed to be many variables, too many variables to consider, or overlook; far too many indeed!

"Maybe I need to sit down and think about this a little more, try to put two and two together before I jump to any conclusions about what might just be a simple over exaggeration," I mentioned to myself as I was trying not to think too hard, maybe I was right; that I was over thinking about what was going on! And what was really going on anyway? Believe you me, I will get to the bottom of this, I can't let my friend's disappearance go unnoticed, nor can I let those responsible get away with this!

GONE FISHIN'

[I'll be back shortly kids, until then please enjoy a short message from our sponsors]

[PAGE INTENTIONALLY LEFT BLANK]

[PAGE INTENTIONALLY LEFT BLANK]

INEFFABLE: "What's That Mean?"

(I Can't Explain That Here)
(:8:)

> This feeling ... A ventured reeling ... Spinning back ... On my heels ... I'm ready to be done ... I have yet still to begun! ... Faster than you can say ... The sentences of which have past ... you will realize I have won...

> When two worlds collide ... Which would you rather be on? ... Me ... I'd rather be lost in space when that happens ... That way ... I cannot hear anyone scream ... And I'm too far away to care!...

> Caught In a Maelstrom

  o   Caught in a maelstrom ... Feeling just like a bum ... Going from drum to drum ... Just to feel your warmth ... But it gets cold too fast ... This feeling will not last ... Why must I be out classed ... By those clearly under me? ... Someday I will regain ... My title and my reign ... But for now I bide my time ... For they will slip away ... Just like a summer's day ... And with them goes their warmth ... But darling do not fret ... Just forget them yet ... I will light a drum for two! ...

➢ They Call Me Mellow Yellow

      o   Into the trouble ... The boiling bubble ... There once was a fellow ... He was all yellow ... He was super mellow ... But his temper was ... Not! ... They used to tease him ... They used to poke him with rods ... You cannot imagine how many rods they had to find around town ... I mean people were starting to rename their kids' "Rod" just to keep up with demand ... It's crazy to think of what that must do to the child ... I mean, here you are ... Knowing your name is Susan ... Or something other than Rod ... And then all of a sudden, you are being called "Rod" ... And being forced head first into some guy over and over again till you break! ... Then being tossed aside and replaced by someone else ... Could be your friend ... Could be your enemy ... But regardless of the circumstances of your particular relationship ... You have become a drone ... Merely a pawn in this field ... This vortexual plane of existence ... Does your own life affect others? ... Is there always a give and a take? ... If you lived an isolated existence and did nothing but self-serving activities ... Would you still affect those around you in the same way as if you actively engaged in community events? ... Does the butterfly effect work on blind principles? ... Or does it have a more direct and personal consequential outcome? ... That is to say ... If I sneeze in a cave while never having any actual contact with the outside world in any way, shape, or form ... Would that somehow cause the market in china to crash in the same, or similar, manner as if I actively made an effort to cause said crash? ... For that matter ... What is in the "secret sauce?" What indeed!? ...

➢ Clueless

o   Unexplainability is the sense that one cannot control the world around oneself. That simply there are forces a foot that make the vast plane we occupy all the more bewildering to the untrained eye; that which views what seems to be a gross understatement of reality. There are too many variables to consider when one uses the bathroom, let alone flies into space and attempts to control the limitless emptiness that, ironically, occupies reaches not fully understood. However, we know, or think so, more about the small portion of visible sky in space than we do our own oceans! ...

➢ Plastic On The Attack

o   I bleed from my ears ... Like a river of tears ... Weeped from the heart ... Don't let me start! ... There is a forest inside ... To which I reside ... There will be no one ... Except for the son ... That sees me as I am ... But then there is them ... The ones that call ... Damn them all! ... They found me at last ... For all the time that has past ... There is only one reason to go on ... But she is long gone! ... So I stagnate ... And relate to the water in my pond ... I'm fond of the frond that grows there ... But a lily would prove to brighten up my forest ... The one within the trees ... Up the stalks, walk past her knees ... Bends with the bees ... Oh shall I tell you stories ... About them flowers and things ... Those birds with wings? ... Magic that gives rise to surprising developments? ... Let us be assured to that ... Seated in the grandness of the village people ... There is a barber ... A baker ... And a candlestick ... Shaker ... "It goes a-rat-a-tat-tat when I hit it like that!" ... Now what kind of toy does a sound that way? ... The only kind of toy that is too costly to say! ...

➢ Amazingly Un-amazed

o   There are many fast-friends ... Like the food of the same name ... They are good for a smile ...

Three "mmm's" and you're full for a while ... But clogged are your arteries ... At least then ... Your rest-assured ... That your vision could be blurred ... And your heart stead-fast ... Left as stationary ... Inside a cast ... Pine or wood ... But then you could ... Be free at last ... To live without ... The fear of doubt ... That pains the cause ... There never was ... And no one shows this side to you ... Fake are smiles ... Stuck like glue ... All is a play ... But all for you ... So feel safe ... Because you are the star ... They all know ... Just who you are! ...

➤ Board

o Board ... In a house of cards ... Made of glass ... Toppling over with class ... There is nowhere to go except up ... Or so they say when you are at the bottom ... But you could always grab a shovel ... And dig yourself a whole new level ... The closer you get to the white noise within ... The further from feeling to which you are dealing ... The better you could feel! ... As you sit with the complimentary crackers and cheese wheel ... That goes with your whine! ...

➤ Tune A Fish

o One fish ... Two fish ... Red fish ... Blew fish ... Wait-wait-wait! ... I thought you knew fish ... You didn't do fish! ... Did you? Ha-ha-ha, no ... You're a true fish ... I kid you! ...

➤ Truck Style

o Evil engines ... On my back ... They rear up ... For the attack ... Timeless trials ... We see host ... There is nothing ... left to boast! ... The way we see ... The world this day ... The ways our eyes ... Come carry away ... The story line ... Is inside you ... The story is written ... To be true! ...

➤ Forchin 500

o Delicious is the flava ... Hot-hot is the motion ... A destroyer is the vessel ... I'm the commander in Dis Ocean! ... Sending out the fleet ... When the seas get rough and tumble … Don't you worry … I will not stumble! … You might get wet without a slicker … But fasten your seat belt … Before I redline this sticker … Fresh off the block … First to cross the line … Victory sweeter … Than raspberry wine … Understand if you can … But I'd much rather make dolla's! … "Keep your pennies for da calla's!" …

➤ The Key Ingredient Is, Gravy

o In a biscuit sea … There is nothing more to be … You either swim at home … Or else you swim alone … These times I live … My life … I give … Is yours to own! … You're in the zone … And i-i-i-i-i-i! … Oh, I am here! … Here for you! … Yes you, my dear! … It is true … And you know that … Oh yes … You know that! … But does it show? …

➤ Bread?

o Sandwiched inside my mind … Where is the plate? … I cannot find … You are there … Without me … Mayo … Mustard … I cannot see … The pictograph … That I read inside my head … There are visions that speak … And cause me dread! … Explode their noise in colorful poise … There was a note … It said, "Hello!" … But there is no forwarding address … And no caller to re-ring … So I bid a farewell … And a Hollyday … For the lily is in season … But the sales are not well…

➤ People … Just Read It

o Random people … Random lines … Random problems … But all the same whines … You wake up and look in the mirror but you only see me … Or as close as your mind can be … You blink, once … Twice … But I'm all there is … You sit right down, and pull on your hair … Thinking back, at how you could dare … It's almost as if, you didn't even care! …

➤ Where am I? … The town of "No", that's where … How I got there … Is a mystery to me … Was anyone looking or did I just "be?" ... It is said, that one day I appeared ... Clothed and polished, I even had a beard! ... There were no lines, drawn in the sand ... Only those, in the palm of my hand ... I asked those questions ... That many have before ... Only this time, I asked them to the door ... In my face it slammed, by everyone in town ... Even by Bobo, the super friendly clown! ... Then one day, I just sat down ... I'm not gonna ask again, I'm tired of the lies ... Everyone says "No!" They are starting to despise! ... I guess it's almost time to go ... My welcome is all through ... I will not need my shades this time ... Because where I'm going is nice and cool! ...

➢ After Hours

o Awake ... At night, I hear the flight ... Of the birds ... They come at dawn ... To take away the pain ... Just like the rain ... There is no more ... Nothing more ... That can come from the crying ... But the pain is just too much ... It feels like dying ... You don't know ... But you go ... You go without me ... But I stop you ... I say "No, there is no more!" ... There is only that big door ... But you stop me too ... And you say "No, there is more ... There are clothes in the store!" ... And we can fix this ... But I fight back ... On the attack ... And what is left of my esteem! ... For myself! ... I fight hard ... But you win by my accord ... Because I let you ... Even though I did not want too! ... Because it was my turn to win this time ... So sorry ... I said sorry ... Did you not hear me the first time? ... I hit the bubble and moved my piece ... And landed on your head ... So back home you go ... I hope you are not dead! ... Or out for revenge ... They say it's best served cold ... And it's mighty cold outside ... So the vengeful should not hide! ... But be out there ... With a sweater and a hat ... Just like that cat ... Someone had a bone to pick with him ... Just as long as it's not chicken ... Because it might harm him ... Or is that only dogs? ... The hot ones I like best ... Well, better than the rest ... In France they eat frogs ... Or just the legs ... Whereas in Philly, it's raw eggs! ... Or a sandwich made of cheese steak ... But make no Miss steak ... There will be consequences when you're done ... But this is all for fun! ... Because the benefit is set ... But it benefits no one! ... And it's your turn to move! ...

- ➢ Orange Grove
  - o   Into the orange grove ... The rabbit did call to me ... As I follow I ponder once ... "Why am I taller than that tree?" ... And so it would seem that I'm shrinking fast ... Into this field of dreams! ...
- ➢ Event
  - o   Bored ... Time going slowly down the drain ... Liquid plumber on the brain! ... I feel sick ... I must refrain ... From this dock ... She is going crazy ... So off I walk ... I'm feeling lazy ... Till I hear a knock ... Tip-toes past my door ... Two shakes ... I'm off the floor...
- ➢ Price ... Is Precious
  - o   Rhinos in a field of grace ... Wearing lace ... They tip-toe ... Without a trace ... You never knew ... Such creatures like I do ... They want you ... To be inept too ... Just like ... The Cleave-land Zoo ... For when they are running ...Around like a clown ... They run tricks ... And do their trading around town ... So you see ... That is why the price of ivory ... Out shines the price of gold ... Because only fortune favors the bold! ...
- ➢ Gameboy
  - o   Just out the shower ... Raising up my power! ... Going for the gold ... Gonna beat it in an hour ... Less with a mushroom ... Gonna get my zoom-zoom ... Then coming back ... In time for a light spoon ... After I grind down ... I will get ready for the town...
- ➢ Order ... Isn't The Law
  - o   Reading up the pages ... On the book report tonight ... 60 minutes ... Is all that's left to fight ...

There he goes again ... He just dropped off the chart ... All these pictures I see ... Are less than works of art! ... You call me on the phone at night ... I look inside the mirror ... And know that's not right ... It's one o'clock in the world somewhere ... Maybe here ... Or maybe there ... "I want a bald rabbit ... Now!" "I'm sorry Madam ... They said they have no hare." ... "How do you dare defy me ... This I swear! ... Bring me what I request ... Or so help me ... I will digest!" ... "Perhaps I mistook their words my lady ... I thought I heard a rabbit sound in the background ... But it did sound shady!" ...

➤ Rodger

o   Art dodger in the field of pain ... I see through the clouds ... But the world is clouded with rain ... Dirty paint ... Orange sun ... You look to me ... To guaranty your fun ... I will not speak ... Unless spoken too ... But ... Will you? ... The time it takes to cook my potato ... In the microwave ... Should be shorter than the time I wait for an answer to my cries ... This city ... Of cities ... Is full of lies! ... Riddle me this ... Your order is up ... But you didn't order these fries! ... But who did? ... One of them? ... Those guys? "There is no one else here!" ... Said the mirror...

➤ Days

o   The beginning of the end of days is twilight ... Leads to night ... which is only the beginning of the day ... It's said that it's darkest just before the dawn ... The days ... Though they seem so long ... It's the night that which continues on ... The conscious unconsciousness of those who see the light ... Are the incessant those that proclaim what is right? ... But you cannot understand that which has no roots in reality! ... For the inability to see ... Does not itself proclaim to be unseen! ...

➤ Eel

o   I spice my eel sunny side up! ... Like my eggs from the cup ... You look at me ... Round table two

... They sit and stair right at you! ... In the dining room ... All draped in blue ... Was it mustard ... With the wrench? ... Just give me a Clue ... I will kick your Life ... Then play Sorry soon! ... Trouble with the bubble is double ... Like Jeopardy ... Only my fortune is not rounded ... Like that wheel ... Sounds like a steal to me ... So just pollenate that stamen ... Or could it be? ... The simple tasks are not as e-z ... As they seem ... For as you wake ... There is reminiscence of a stream! ... Like Mars in your pants ... Red dirt is best for plants! ... Can you really understand 'cepts' I say? ... They are not 'con's that speak! ... Some of the words are not for the meek! ... Even though, they can inherit ... Meaning ... But to keep it, will take merit! ...

> Focus Pokus

   o   In my mind I see the truth I lay behind ... The numbered walls that fall for me ... Only live beyond the trees ... You look inside the dark light sky ... And all you seem to do is fly! ... Inside yourself ... Yet outside the walls ... These barriers that nary fall ... They always seem to heed the call ... To coincide ... Yet bury them all ... There once was lost ... What I have found ... No one is clearer than the clown ... The painted face says it all ... Who are you to bluff his call? ... Inside I see ... What you hide from me ... Like a present yet to be ... To those that are not yet ready ... All is good in be you see ... So what does all this have to do ... Lesser such than that with me? ... All that is ... Or ever were ... Will the clock strike down in plural? ... When you ride the coaster whirl ... Do not focus or you'll hurl! ...

> 1

   o   Ornamental fun land ... Drifting off in dreams ... There is but a small man ... Appearing in the streams ... "Off you go," he says now ... Off you go indeed! ... There is much more snow hear ... Much too much to feed ... There will be a rain storm ... There will be some time above ... The reasons of the trials fought ... The reasons for the pain it brought ... There will be too much to know ... There will be nowhere to go! ... I will see you there you know ... And no one will know how to sew! ... The dictator has eyes on you ... With his gaze ... His aim is true! ... There will be no one else to sue ... But there will be the magic man ... The game plan is set to screw ... The time it takes for us to do ... There will not be a soulless shoe ... One by one there is the field ... One by one they will not yield ... There was a master plan I stealed ... But then it blew away my friend ... There once was two young mice at hand ... One was furry ... One was bland ... They called each other 'Lad' ... But just a tad ... And they always played tennis in the nude ... But seconds went by ... And then minutes were had ... No one suspected the scurrying cad! ... There he was ... There he went ... Off by the door and out with a stint! ...

➤ Flys in oil ... Start to boil ... I watch them run ... While I hold my gun ... Off in the distance ... I see the salvation I was waiting on ... Till you hear the sound of the gong ... Stay silent ... Stay still ... For one day soon ... It will be yours to kill! ...

➤ I seal this locket ... From behind ... The clasp is plastic ... You will find ... The pain I feel ... Is all in my mind ... Or that is ... What they have told me ... But I feel it's true ... Only ... If they are in my mind too! ...

➤ Silence is golden ... For I'm told ... But I have been quiet for a while ... Though I'm still poor! ...

➤ A clean slate ... Starts with the bait ... One must string the hook ... But careful ... The prey is starting to look ... Play your cards right ... And they will bite ... One move wrong ... And the prey is gone! ... You have to understand my friend ... That this could be the end! ... I don't mean to do you wrong ... But you know ... This is my favorite song ... I have to get ... To the prey first

... Or else this day ... Of days ... Could be your worst! ... The interesting thing of all ... Is that you already told me ... You would take the fall ... And now here you are ... Trying to be the best ... I've already won ... So this is now your test ... Could you have beaten me ... If you weren't just my life vest? ...

➢ Into the air ... My mind does float ... Like an airship micro-boat! ... I look at you ... With a blanketed stare ... Into the chasm ... That supports your hair ... The frost that flows ... From your eyes ... Catches me ... Sort of by surprise ... I ponder justly ... As I ponder aloud ... Where did you get enough people for this crowed? ... "Just lying around" ... A voice from within is heard ... As if they were Leg-ohs ... And that was the word ... My very existence is halted ... For the moment to stand ... And wonder ... By whose hand ... Did this craziness happen? ... Like a fire ... Within my brain ... The nerves are firing ... Bullets that strain! ... The miss-connection to the destination as thus ... Causes such pain ... And ill trust! ... I do not assume to ease it lightly ... The pain lets me know I'm still alive ... For when I die ... I should arrive ... The pain will be there ... But physically it will not ... Only a memory condensed in thought! ... Time is a factor I have little of ... The major reason is ... I'm all out of love! ... No! ... Wait! ... That's not it! ... Time is relative they say ... Just like how you can never get the time of day! ... Unless you ask a relative ... Who will simply just give it away ... But everyone else just says ... "No!" Ok? ...

➢ The right way ... Merely a subject of perception ... Right and wrong have about as much of a meaning as do right and left ... Up, down, and sideways ... Can there be such a thing as a cardinal right, while simultaneously conveying that there is also a correctness value to this? ... Speaking merely controversial, there could be both an occurrence of right and wrong while left is spliced

somewhere between both forms of the right measure ...
But there is a third factor that must be demonstrated in
this concept ... View ... Sight has a strange way of playing the odds for ... Or against us ... It appears that the
only way to truly understand, is to not be able to fully see
from either side ... But have a sort of peripheral vision to
both ... Keeping everything fuzzy could keep everything
clearer in the end! ... Sitting in a room filled with chairs
... All but three of them are facing the "right" way ... All
but three of them are filled first ... Leaving the lonely
few to be filled by those that arrive just moments after the
masses ... So, forced to sit in the "wrong" chairs ... The
late members of the majority hang their heads in shame
... They are made to feel like outcasts in their otherwise
"Perfect society!" ...

> Ducky: hard working party fowl ... He's a good
citizen and he loves to plow ... He works at a farm ... He
even feeds cows ... Yep that's Ducky ... The party fowl
... He was raised in a mansion with a silver spoon ...
They couldn't afford golden ... But they could the moon
... You see, back in those days ... Gold was too rich! ...
Only the super famous could afford cars as long as a bus
... But that didn't stop Ducky ... From making his mark!
... He even surpassed the world's smarted lark! ...

> Self-absorbed ... I cannot spill ... The pain inside
... Is enough to kill ... I look at myself ... In the mirror
... I cannot look ... Any clearer ... The stories I tell ...
To hide the pain ... Are just distractions ... Caused by
my brain ... The type that make you see yourself ... Just
placed up there ... On the shelf ... A tag through your
little ear ... Staring blindly into thin air ... With glass-
eyes ... You see through me ... As if I were made of
glass ... Completely! ... A window ... Through my soul
is felt ... But sooner now ... I have knelt ... To pick me
up, off the shelf ... I bought myself ... For a dollar,
twelve ... That is quite an inflated price! ... I thought ...

However ... It was nice ... I got ... To keep that which ... Should be mine ... For if I'm wrong ... I will find ... That you will be there ... To guide a solution ... Because all that I feel inside ... Is nothing but pollution ... A sickness I know ... Deep down inside ... Is fueling me ... With no place to hide ... Pouring out of me ... Like a river of hate ... Filling me ... Like you on our first date! ...

➤ I look at myself now ... As I sit here and wonder ... What was it all for ... Or is this merely a blunder ... Should I be here? ... Or am I there in reality? ... Is this real? ... Or really just within me? What I see ... Could this be? ... Something tangible? ... Or just like what's on TV? ... I don't know how to cope with what is real ... These are the same questions I ask ... When I cop a feel! ...

➤ Third-eye blind

o   That which I cannot hide ... But the pain inside ... I can't see ... What becomes me ... You understand me not! ... For what I lack ... You have got ... In the mind ... There is the few ... The lucky ones ... That are not you! ... If I eat ... The sweet-sweet meat ... I will in fact ... Bestow a treat ... Those of you ... Who follow me ... Shall ... For now on ... Be held to see ... That you will be ... The chosen ones to flee ... Scared of fire ... Yet born of ashes ... That are new ... You look asunder ... At us two ... In the light castle ... There is no grey ... When the soul searching ... Runs astray ... Little does ... The children play ... For the amount ... That there is left ... In the day ... I sit and say ... Hooray! ...

➤ Great players are we ... The ones that jest ... To control the sea ... The old man blows ... A great many ... Curtains away ... But not until ... This fine-fed day ... Alas I call ... And vast be the winds ... To be the shelter ... Of mine kin's ... Into the outside ... I call from within ... The journey is ending ... Before it begins! ...

➤ Into the crevasse ... Come calling me now ... The wild card plays ... And a chance to win ... I wonder now ... How it will begin ... The story I call ... From within my own mind ... Might be too much ... And make me go blind...

➤ If I were to stand up ... And cry ... Would you be there ... To cover up my lie? ... Could you hold ... The truth at bay? ... Could save me ... For another day? I sit here ... And bar these tears of mine ... I chance to stop ... The recurring whine ... The pain I feel ... I live with now ... Never waving ... Nor ever staving ... My constant turmoil ... I feel today ... Never is it ... Less I say ... I always hurt ... Yet feel fine! ... Chaos too ... Draws such a line ... Halfway from perfect ... But perfectly unreal ... I only wish ... I could have more time to steal! ...

➤ A penny for your thoughts ... They say ... Is that British style ... Or USA? ... I don't know ... Which I have been led to believe ... But my thoughts ... Are worth as much as to me ... As my sleeve! ...

➤ Into the darkness I wish I were ... The pain that I feel begins to blur ... The constant openness that surrounds me ... Starts to mess with my head ... The pain subsides ... And I feel half dead ... It seems to me ... That life can be ... Nothing more than a possibility! ... The half-lived truth ... That is this way ... The sadness ... Left to another day ... I feel them all ... When I'm at rest ... As if this all ... Is one big test ... The answers are there ... To my despair! ...

➤ Like a thousand drums ... Beating in unison ... Singing a song that is never done ... Playing a pity dance to my soul ... Never ending ... Never droll ... The repeating beat calls my name ... The song is catchy ... Yet tame ... I cannot control the feelings I have! ...

➤ I can see through your disguise ... Right there waiting beyond my eyes ... Things that haunt me that you

can't see ... Are more real now ... Than ever should be!
...

> The day has been ran ... The clowns have finally passed on into the night ... And the dog of 'ell will return one day ... To reclaim his land that was taken so mercilessly ... By the king of the damned that so rule the underworld that is his own domain! ...

> Well, kiddies ... The son of the few that were led here to die hath fallen into the pool of evil light ... And now ... As well as forever ... Will be turned into what he has tried so very hard to stop ... And now he is thirsty for the blood of the ones that have put him into such a state of never-ending turmoil ... That must always remain in order ... To keep order stable and just in this day and age! ...

> Orange zest fully clean I am ... To be in the tree pot stem ... Into the mirror my stairs they know ... And onward ... Upward ... And inward I go ... To the cherry type dressing here in the hall ... I see more of her than of them all ... I beg her pardon ... And snap pictures with my mind ... My picture printer is of the imaginary kind ... But ponder this I do at all ... Ripe-type skin ... But the stem will be my fall ... The sensuality I hold ... In my nose it feels cold ... You are me ... In my mind I see ... That you must be with me to be ... The total recall of the sum at all ... Is to be last ... As I am tall ... The makers of the game of Life ... Obviously needed one ... But soon I will understand why they called it fun! ... The page of life ... That I am on ... Is not written ... But it is a song ... One I have forgotten now ... But the entire chorus ... Is hymned by the town cow! ...

> In the middle of the field there was a boy ... Stood there with his ball ... And called unto the world to blind the sun ... Which gets into the boys eyes ... "The world is cruel!" ... Said the man ... That drove the boy to his standing ground up top the hill ... And the eyes look

upon him yet again ... Questions roll from the tongue of man ... And then the answers flood like a river run dry ... They never knew what was in the pudding ... And never would find out ... Till they all dropped like flies in the soup of life ... That we tread every day as we get up to fight a war against sleep ... And the sand man ... Who is living within all of us ... The standard response for the visions deep within ... We hide from during the day ... Is to just work ... And work until we die ... And the visions take back over to rerun our lives ... In stereo ... But without sound ... As heard by the depth man in all of us ... The visions I see ... And speak of ... With these hands I torture you with this day ... Are but without feeling ... And remorse to speak of ... I control my own sanity ... By the volume that I speak with ... By the handles on the wall I padded myself ... I understand that the milk man comes at noon ... But our milk is delivered by six in the morning ... And is emptied again by five that next day ... I looked at my fridge ... And asked it why the milk was gone ... And it responded that I should pay double the fine ... And get the extra creamy cheese that comes with my order ... For it's the supper rich and fulfilling type of blend ... I looked into its cold-steel eyes ... And I knew where they took her! I'm tearing myself apart ... From the inside out ... The pieces fall ... And there is no doubt ... I cannot understand myself ... And I cannot hear you cry for help ... The way you look ... And the stance you peel. The understanding that I feel ... You look into my eyes at last ... And the time is past for me to leave ... But I cannot go ... I do not know ... I cannot feel ... But of the stair from the crow ... You look at the wall I padded ... And ask the difference I added ... For the walls at the hospital do not have buttons at all ... You stand there and cheerily act like you care for me ... But I can see deep into your eyes ... And I know the truth ... That you speak these lies ... And disguise your sense of understanding ...

Which I speak to you about in the corner of my eyes ... The morning comes and goes ... And finally I see the sparking of the rose outside the door ... I lean there and more is heard from the wind ... The answer I have been waiting on ... Finally blew in from the coast ... The tide is near ... And finally clear ... Is the vision I have seen all along ... The picture I have seen ... And the yearning of clean meat is here ... And lastly my dear ... I have been acquitted of the crime of loving you all this time ... I grab for the sun ... But closer still is my cinnamon bun ... So I eat in the morning ... To fulfill my destiny ... Because I reached for what I could see ... The moment is here ... And come lastly ... I sear the beef on the radio dial ... Five minutes on one side ... And the other takes a while ... You ask me to call your face ... but all I can call you with ... Is my mace! ...

I Think It's Called Moby's Dick

"I'm Male-ish, Call me"
("Whales, MMM, Sperm Whales")
(:9:)

➢ There stands before me ... That which I know all too well ... Aye ... It be the fish I see ... That which long John ... Himself ... Could never catch ... Nor batter and fry ... Then serve with a side of chips! ... You call me as if you know me ... And I know you do not at all! ... But you think I don't know ... This little fact at hand ... So you blind-side me ... With questions ... And the so-called ... Self-assured answers ... You repeat to me ... As if you rehearsed them ... In front of the mirror ... "Two days left and I'm off to the market!" ... Said the beef shank on my thigh ... I looked puzzled ... But carried on by ... Standing in the field of my dreams ... I look down ... And ask what manner of speech does my body possess ... To the answer I was waiting ... I must stress ... That the answer I was given ... Was merely the best! ... You see my friend ... That merely my leg meat

143

wanted out ... So a prison break was ordered at last ... A written test ... I nearly passed ... I walk about the floor ... At night ... Looking ... Seeking ... Hunting for a bite ... You hide away ... And look for cover ... But do not worry ... I'm your number one lover! ... Secret plays in mysterious ways ... And you know the plan ... That would make me your man ... But you play your cards ... To the point that I fail ... To see that you're a fox ... With two tales ... Sonic ... The hedgehog ... Is missing his buddy ... For she is right here ... Beating me in rummy! ... I make my plans ... And stick right to them ... But no one can prepare ... For the act of mayhem! ... Chaos is deceiving ... While you act calm and collective ... Your mind is racing ... And pacing your perspective ... You think you see the cat ahead ... But all you notice ... Is the pile you dread ... The head of marketing ... And play-rights assurance ... The day is just a light occurrence ... The ridiculous spectacle ... Of magic and benevolence ... Is only halted ... By the act of violence! ...

➢ Into the forest ... The river runs ... Following closely ... The creeper stuns ... Inch by inch ... Gets nearer still ... For one short day closer ... Of you I kill ... Tiny cans ... A plenty they are ... The far off places ... Burn bright like a star ... The stairwell calls my name ... And hither runs ... The tails left there ... By the suns ... You answer my phone calls ... With Chantilly lace ... Too bad for me ... You cannot see my face ... I look at you ... Through the phone at last ... And I realize ... My time has passed ... The morning has come and gone ... the time to weep ... Has been too long ... You look in the past ... As you always do ... And one day ... I will too ... But until that day ... Is here at last ... I must tell you ... To stand fast ... The market is ever growing ... Slowly showing ... That one day you will be mine! ...

➢ Click-click-click ... The light turns on ... Then I start with my little song ... Hmm-hmm-hmm ... Would you help me and sing along? ... I wonder who there has the gong ... One and two ... Skip to my lue ... I hear a church bell ... Swing a clue ... I look to my left ... And I see you ... You look at me ... And send a smile or two ... I smile back ... And wave at you ... To come here ... And have a seat ... won't you? ...

> ➤ Negligent Auto National Selebration Association *[NANSA]*, where gramars/pellin DOESN'T not count ... Thant's write, whe'a're also dislectical too!'?.

o   Fried chicken used to stand for things back in the day! ... I once called over to Uncle Sam and asked for a ride to the mall ... And he was like "Sure ... But you should really re-think my proposal of getting a job" ... And I was like, "Sure dude," but I would never call him dude ... I simply nodded and told him I needed new pants ... You know, for this job thing I am supposed to get ... "What is it, like a chia pet or something?" ...

> ➤ 27 Reasons ... Or maybe 26

o   It was the best of times ... It was the worst of times ... So that must make it mediocre times...

o   The little Engine that would, and on occasion, did ... Because if he could, then he should! ...

o   The man with the deer stands alone inside his house ... All are watching, except for the mouse ... Stepping outside he goes ... Changed are his features, and his clothes ... Stepping lightly, like pixies he does ... One by one, his feet venture toward where the deer once was ... As he approaches, the deer notices thus ... And outstretched his arms become as must ... Corn appears, and does flock the deer ... Toward his front, not his rear ... Calmly they eat ... These treats brought forth ... Calmly, too calmly, but of course ... Out from behind the man, appears, a monkey with an evil glare ... A shotgun with a trigger set to a hair ... A cry is heard, a shot without a word ... And one dead deer, that saved, no one could! ...

     o   I'm so alone right now ... My heart is beating ... But I can't feel it ... All I know ... Is I'm slipping away ... Slowly dying ... Because you're not in my life ... I know you love me ... But you don't show ... Where oh where ... Did you ever go? ... I sit here waiting on a sign ... Perhaps ... I might be witness ... To something divine ... An intervention is in order ... Perhaps ... You could come on over ... But alas ... You will not ... I always have to make a trot ... I love to see you ... As much as I can ... But nothing is scheduled in the plan ... I hate you ... To say you love another ... I hate you ... To say you're with the others ... But there is nothing I can do ... I am not ... There with you ... I wish you would ... Just tell me the truth ... Of what you do ... Don't spare me details ... If it's all true ... baby-baby-baby ... You drive me crazy! ...

     o   Inside I'm hollow ... Tormented and twisted ... Poked ... Prodded ... Tasted ... And wasted ... I yearn for knowledge ... And burn with desire ... I know nothing of the outside realm ... Only of the heat of the fire ... I care of nothing ... And the unknown I be ... The door to escape what I see ... The inside holds a safer place ... One with a caring embrace ... I run from the terror inside ... The best thing for me ... Is just to hide ... I hold close my pillow ... And blink but once ... Watchful glance ... But not too much ... I see these things ... As clear as day ... Some of you ... Might even say ... These things ... To me ... Are as real as can be ... But listen close ... And watch to see ... What you notice ... Is all in your head ... Those things ... That you said ... You saw ... That were dead ... Soon here I see ... That these things really be ... And somehow ... They have spotted me ... They watch me close ... And stare very deep ... I must act quick ... And without a peep ... To gather my

soul ... And the rest of my being ... I must make a run ...
And start my fleeing ... For the door to my room ... Is
locked from within ... I cannot find the key ... Through
all of my sin ... The challenge now ... Is how to end ...
The wonders ... Of a different bend ... I cannot continue
... My fight ... Someday ... I fear I might ... Stare deeply into the eyes ... Of those things ... That I see ... That
seem like the crows ... They just watch you closely ...
From far away ... Waiting patiently ... Until that time ...
That you drop dead ... And clear the way ... For the
crows to feast ... For at least one more day! ...

> Into the void ... Beyond the tower of the Noid ...
The walls I see ... Speak only to me ... The ears they
speak of ... Are held together ... By stalks they reek of
... The stench of death ... Fills my nostrils full and tight
... A wink of the curtain's call ... The walls shake ...
And I know it all ... The story of my life is ending ...
And time around me is bending ... Get out before the
church bells cry ... The eagles flock around me ... And
the crows start to party ... The time to call the meeting is
in order ... The book is opened ... And the pages set ...
The last one written as of yet ... The rooms I used to toy
and play... Sooner still must fade away ... The ball room
classes fade from light ... And soon I realize that you
were right ... The light from the moon ... That flickers
from the sun ... Struggles longer one by one ... The picture studded ... And cast in stone ... Must be set there all
alone! ...

> Spiraling down a desert highway ... I stop mid
turn and look to see ... Standing there admiring me ... Is
strangely me ... For what I can see ... Seeing me back is
the aforementioned me ... As well as ... Stopping himself to look and be ... Me that isn't ... But is ... I shall
call "B" ... And as such ... There and standing sound ...
B comes running bound ... "Halt!" I whisper ... Loud
and proud ... Mocking the bird ... That is bald in a crowd

... B said, "Hi, and by the by, how are you my shadow twin?" ... "Care to spill the beans as to your win?" ... *[Ninja-skill-tingle]* As I mingle and shout ... The twin within knows what this is about ... That this is wrong ... But singing alone with the notes of the song ... I can't help but wonder if this really is right ... To delight in the challenge of self-denial ... But could he ... Which then is so be it me ... Win in a trial? ...

> ➤ Boom

    ○   As you stand there in the corner and watch the people go by. Listen very closely and watch them start to die. You first Witness confusion and panic, it will pass. But oh do be careful, that is very deadly gas. Interesting as the concept of homicide may be; you must really have trust, that I will not do anything to hurt you, unless you hurt me! Once a day the mice come to play, they frolic around, and jump up and down. Then one day you come to find, someone trapped them, but they were not as kind. As a fly is sat on a wall somewhere, I hear a trap set in despair; there is a hunt out on the loose, to catch that poor fly in a crude noose. Rhyme with reason, sneezin' to boot; I sometimes where a fancy suit! But alas, it is all for loss; for I have no one but the Winchester from the boss. He said, "Look kid, here you go, one day you might need it; heck you never know." As I look at the barrel, how shiny I think, how white those walls are; they could use a touch of pink! So I lift up the weapon by the handle as such, I point it out, and adjust it as much. I say a few words as a clergy would, then I count back from ten, as I contemplate if I should. When one is reached I say goodbye, sorry the world cannot watch me die! ...

> ➤ Animal Crackers

    ○   ... So then, what are you doing right now?

    ○   "Talking to you while eating animal crackers."

o   Oh, which is your favorite?

o   "You."

o   Ah, how sweet thanks, glad I could reign above the African lion, all be it he is the king of the cracker world, but alas, I have but one thing he has not...

o   "You was about what are you doing, and I don't know to your question."

o   Darn, I guess the lion really does have his day, but merely for this day; I will win my turn yet!

o   "Why do you want to be best?"

o   Of the herd, well that's an easy one, so I can lead an army of unstoppable animal crackers into a frenzy the world has never seen. No one would suspect the seeming docility, and incredible deliciousness, of the wild cracker crocs that reside in that little box of trickery ... No one, but I! ... The one who shall lead them to the Promised Land, where they can bathe in milk and live happy carefree crackery lives they were made to live ... Do you see, Can you see?

o   "I thought you guys couldn't take drugs."

o   What are you taking about? They are merely crackers. I mentioned nothing of drug use, why do you ask?

o   "You're acting like a crack head."

o   Nah, Just because I want to lead an unstoppable army of bite size crackers, in the delicious shapes of the world's animals, on a frenzy that will bring the world to its knees; does not in anyway suggest drug use, does it?

o   "You don't know what you're talking about."

o   But I do, I have it all planned out. First, I must gain the trust of the African lion and his mistresses. Only then can I begin my plan.

o   "Ok."

o   You don't believe me do you?

o   "I think u need a therapist."

o   Huh, Why?

o   "You are talking crazy."

o   Nah, It's quite possible. Was Napoleon crazy when he opened his bakery? Was Michael Angelo crazy when he and his other brother turtles came together to form up against shredder along with their rat mentor ... Master Splinter?

o   "Yes dear."

o   So you say they were huh?

o   "Stop arguing!"

o   I see, no faith that a simple man with a seemingly difficult plan could ever gain the trust of the most ruthless of all cracker creatures, the dreaded African lion!?

o   "Ok."

o   So you finally believe that I can do it do you?

o   "Sure but you got to get your own bag boy."

o   Oh, but I have many.

o   "Great."

o   But every time I try to gain their trust they seem to argue as if they feel jealous that I have the power to unite them. So I dispose of the kingdom and start anew. And bag after bag they have grown smarter to my advances.

o   "*[Whack]* Snap out of it."

o   Soon I fear they will stand up to me and unite themselves against my might; if that is their way, be sure I will be ready. Stand and fight is their way, or forever be crushed and crumbled to the doom.

o   "You have a lot of free time huh?"

o   Why do you say that?

o   "Learn to eat them you're wasting good crackers."

o   Oh, but I do eat them, at least the ones who oppose me. This is why I have so many boxes to this day...

➢ If you want to read my soul ... Climb on down into this hole ... It's quite deep ... And not so narrow ... Don't forget to bring a sparrow ... Careful when you light the lamp lit tires ... Watch careful ... As your sparrow expires! ... You don't have much time ... But do not haste ... Read as much ... Or just a taste ... All before you are lain to waste ... Because your existence is now tied to mine ... The sparrow keeps track of your time ... For if it dies before you leave ... You will not be too far behind ... So call ahead ... To secure your place in line!
...

➢ Eyes

o   Eyes wide open ... But I can't see ... I can feel them ... Stare at me ... Their eyes burn ... With unspeakable pain ... The visions hurt me ... Inside my brain ... I scream inside ... For them to leave me alone ... But they all act ... As if there is no one home ... No one to call on ... When I need them the most ... Only to act ... As if I were their host ... I plead and cry ... And whine and wail ... But nobody there ... To head a sail ... To come to my call ... Or to put up at all ... I speak of these things in me ... These things I see ... That Haunt my soul ... And the depths like a mole...

➢ Facts

o   Half way to heaven ... But closer to hell ... I rot in this body ... I call a cell ... The stories told by me ... Are fact ... At least as recalled ... By my own tact ... Inside of all of us ... Is me ... I am the one you feel ... When you speak to be ... You understand things I say ... Inside your head ... As if you said them ... Back when you were a kid ... You don't know how I got there ... Lately you don't care! ... All you know ... Is you can't recall ... A better time in your life ... Then before I was

151

ruling it ... Beckoning you to be ... To do ... To see ...
You answer the call ... As if I were on TV ... Telling you
to buy this new bike ... It's made to go ... So buy it ...
Now you know you want to try it! ...

➢ FL

o   Life is a meaning less wonder! ... Yeah ...
I wonder why I'm still alive ... Well ... To indulge the
pain ... And further stop the suffering and turmoil ...
Within the very reaches of my soul ... If one would say
that I might even have one anymore ... I think that everything went "Downhill" when I was eight ... Ah ... Those
beautifully innocent years ... The ones that force one to
rethink this view on life in general...

o   For I speak of the time that started ... And
then lead ... To this very bit of literary rubbish ... For my
life has never been full of itself ... So to speak ... True I
have lived a privileged life ... I have never had to work
till I left my home ... I have always had a roof over my
head ... And both parents that care a great deal about me
... But I have never truly been happy with my life ... I
have had happy times ... And joyous occasions ... But all
that was on the outside ... All of that was felt ... Not
from within ... But was shined upon the inside from afar!
...

o   There was only one time in my life where
I have felt so alive as to say that life is meaningful ...
And joyous ... A time to play and frolic ... And have a
marry day ... Only once have I known such beautiful
feelings and thoughts ... Only once was I truly happy ...
Not just on the outside ... But actually within! ... Will I
ever feel that again? ...

o   Sad as it may be to hear such words and
think such thoughts ... But yes ... That is how it once
was ... And as such ... I could not understand these feelings ... And became attached to them ... To a point that I
was co-dependent ... Something I have not been before

... It took a long time to understand them finally ... And I realize my wrong doings! ...

> Follow

o   Do not follow my story with your eyes ... Do not follow my story to your surprise ... I will not follow you home in my disguise ... Or will I? ... I'm just one of those guys! ...

> Forever story

o   In the city I call to thee ... What hath the dawn bring to me? ... In the middle of the night ... I see ... What I cannot see ... And yet they call to me ... From within me ... I can breathe from the trees ... I understand the birds and the bees ... The flowers ... And the decrees that my father left me ... I want to make it so ... And so do we! ... The few that be ... The ones that guard the family ... To be ... Is just to be ... But it's not too easy ... To be the one ... That is the one ... To have the fun ... And not to be the one ... With the gun ... When it's time to run ... Because you ran out of time ... When it's ahead of the crime ... You just sat there and chimed ... Your last rhyme ... When you said hello ... And now you have to go ... And I said to you ... That it's time to roll ... But you just have to know ... That I love you baby! ... I always did ... Even though you have a kid ... And the kid's not mine ... I still will forever time ... Love the alpha bit ... Just as long as you sit in it ... And I am there ... As long as I have clean under where ... That we both can share! ... I will be happy ... As can be ... Just like a tree ... And that brings me back ... To the beginning of this story! ...

> Here them whine ... Here them cry ... Why oh why ... Do they come to me to die? ... I look into ... Their eyes with delight ... As one by one ... I allow them to bite ... Knife them ... I do ... One by one ... And sometimes two ... I run the water ... To clean the wounds

... For nightfall is soon ... The shadows return ... To reap their fill ... Taking count for all that I kill! ...

➤ Only speak ... For what I do ... I silence that ... Which causes me too ... I answer for ... What I think aloud ... Staying quiet ... To fool the crowd ... They do not ... Need to know ... What one day ... Will end this show! ...

➤ I wake up quite early today ... And I have the faintest reply you say ... "That once the day is gone, to-day slips into yesterday!" ... But I simply push you away ... For I must not be late again ... And as I brush my teeth ... And wash my face ... I look into the mirror ... To make quite sure I am not a disgrace ... And as I'm reassured as to my looks ... I walk outside to read aloud ... And noticed quickly there is no crowd ... So angered, and outright enraged I am ... I look quite far ... And there is a fem ... I look inside her narrow eyes ... She shows me love ... But it's a disguise ... One I knew I should not idolize! ... But dearly departed ... Who here farted!? ...

➤ Pay attention to what you read ... Pay attention to the words you bleed ... The cycle of pain ... That the world will remain ... Without pain ... Is punishable ... Under the laws of the brain ... Speak without words ... To hear yourself listen from within ... Understand what you do not now know ... Before you go ... Listen close ... And do not fear ... What I have my dear ... You can-not go on ... With this meter ... Or this song ... The story is lain ... Just like tracks in the brain ... To follow the path ... That is beaten ... And dead ... Is like taking one strait to the head ... If you don't understand ... as for the plans ... To the plan at hand ... The mic is hot ... And I know you thought ... Why not? ... But careful is ... As careful does ... Don't be bitten ... By the buzz! ...

➤ Inky ... Stinky ... Pinky ... Winky ... What time is it? ... Inch that minky ... Orange and blue ... Makes purple too ... If you blink ... You will step on her shoe ... Eat some meat ... chill that seat ... Sit and greet ... The killer feet! ...

➢ I cannot feel my mind inside my brain ... it feels as though I am going completely insane ... Would you join me? ... Could you possibly be? ... Completely insane just like me? ... Are you sure you're like that? ... Wait a minute ... Let me converse with my hat ... Yep I'm sane ... At least when it comes to the workings of my brain...

➢ Eyes wide open but I can't see ... In the world of plenty ... There is but only me! ... The sky does shine ... With such bright blinding darkness ... That causes one to see double in the half-life I live ... Open the doors to your reality and you will see what there is about the world that holds me down ... The sky above me is near the ground ... Scared-wide-open, I shut my eyes ... Still I see them to my surprise ... The visions closer creeping come they do ... They call my names, both one and two ... Spirits rise, and fall alike ... At last I realize my dismay in losing my bike ... The evil inside me stalks the door ... The one leading inside me nevermore ... They look past the shadows, but they can't see ... As I look past them, all I see is me ... The wooded hills and valleys alike ... Stair at me just like a tike ... The toddler stood there at the corner still ... Bald as an eagle, but just as ill ... The country has past up the bill ... To the one that will be ever still ... We start to give, but then take the pill ... Wait a minute, I have to know ... What is the answer you peed in the snow? ... Yellow river, is hear soon now ... All I hear, is words from a cow ... The cost of living is stained in blood ... Like from the mountains, in spring there is a flood ... One side fights to stay alive ... While the other only wants to strive ... To rule over the king-dumb of None ... They keep it going till no side has won ... The evil lies, and tells the truth ... Till no one listening remains a tooth ... Inside their head to bite on the line ... That here again is right on time ... The notes are played on very clean dice ... But then thrown in the dirt by very blind mice ... "Eleven or seven," is shouted when fired ... Though I tried, I did not get hired ... A raise to the stakes must be maid ... For the choice to be laid ... The time is now to act out of the box, but within the triangle at hand! ...

➢ I can see the forest for the trees ... But it can't see me ... Because only potatoes have eyes ... But they live underground ... Moles do too ... But they are blind ... So perhaps ... Potato sight is of the hind...

➢ CURE THE DISEASE? SAVE THE PLANET? EVEN THE SCORE? EXILE?

○ Into the shadows I hide from the light ... That which burns me unconditionally ... I stair into the sun ... To undo what I had undone ... The pain I saw ... I see had won ... The orange stains ... Turn purple ... In the ketchup rain ... That spews forth ... From the neck of remorse ... The easy way to remember the sins of man ... Is to catch the sorrow in a can ... The tails tell the way to run ... The one with double ... Will get the job done ... I can't wait 'till the day I am ... The day to remember where I come from ... The time to react ... Is gone and past ... The room is finally spinning fast ... And I look to the wall ... To call on it all! ...

➢ Interest of science ... But scientifically uninteresting ... I speak for myself ... When I speak to the king ... "The story I tell you is both factually accurate and morally true ... The reason we are here is merely for beer ... You see Sire ... The corner store is empty and through ... So we are asking you ... For your key to the cellar here ... Just in case you refuse ... Do keep in mind ... We are holding your sweet daughter dear ... Captive within the mirror ... Break your silence and we will break her rear!" ...

➢ They say there are only the few that can stand the heat of the fire that play in the sun … But those are merely lies that old people tell … So that younger ones stay away from the flames … So they don't get burned by their own disappointment! …

➢ The future may be yours to decide … But as for me … I must hide … The future is … But a place unknown … The stories tell … Of those that are grown … The eldest of few … That one day will be … But none of them … will soon enough … Be me! …

➢ Aliens attack! … But all is contained within a paper sack … The story at hand … Is all made up … By the man … The letters that speak … For words are just that … The letters placed close enough to interact … But not attract … The friendly ones … Are used alone … The angry ones … Force their way home…

➢ Happenstance

o In the shadow of the night … They come for me … They come to feed on the visions in my mind … Such things they see I cannot re-tell for the sake of the unforgiving nature of their ways … The evil I see inside … Is so unrelenting in its way … That those unprepared for it … Shall be forever scared and tormented by its wrath! …

➢ Blackness filled to the brim … A spar of light flickers by … Followed by many like it into a whiteness so bright it blinds … Then a spot of light brighter still is seen within … A chair is cast and someone sitting in the chair is seen … A pan around the chair reveals a man staring in the position of thinking … An intense thought is felt upon his face as you look into his eyes … After a minute of this, the man sits upright transfixed upon the spot he was staring at … As you look deeper into his eyes finally he blinks … And you notice a reflection in his eyes of a small child resembling the man … Deeper still you stare into his eyes, and you notice the boy is within the confines of a cruel cage ... Scared, the boy looks back at you ... The man blinks again, more intense this time as if to dream ... And when the blink is over, a rush of flames erupts within his eyes ... As you once again see what is there, the cage holds the remains of the boy ... You pan around to see what the man was looking at, what reflection there could be ... Nothing is there but white emptiness! ... You pan back to the man, and it is again just his eyes ... As you pan out to reveal his full figure, he once again goes into the position of thinking ... Never losing focus on the spot he so intensely was reviewing ... Then to black, the world goes...

➤ HAPPY DAY!

[With a twist of Lime]

o   Evil surrounds the light ... Light so strong that it burns with unspeakable turmoil and chaos ... The people keep the light at bay with the thoughts of few that never were ... But always have been ... Part of the future of this life ... That is never in to be "Ran", but all in the "Train of life" to be ... That which will never be reached except in the minds of the few innocent people that carry the shadows into the light to kill the visions of those around us...

o   The evil comes at the time when the mind is most active ... And the outer sounds have ceased by any level ... To which none can explain the sorrow felt ... As the one so called as himself is proclaimed to be victorious as never before...

o   I can see the screams as they are slaughtered ... One by one ... In such horrific ways as to make the blood in the veins of even the strong quiver with each pitiful moan ... And gurgle ... That goes on in this day and age...

o   As the few that feed off the light of nightfall go about their day ... The visions return to run rampant across the plain of existence ... In fields of death and destruction ... Unspeakable in the ways of those so told to the other spectrum of evil ... That no one could believe the "Truth!" ...

o   The "Truth," you ask ... Is found by looking deep into the minds which show most thought ... But without actual thinking involved upon the outer realm of the body ... According to the outer world ... But, the real "Truth," as so spoken ... Can only be found out by the eyes of those who speak such words as thus ... Without reason or remorse...

o   The End...

o   But is it really? ... For one must look around and ask thyne self ... Can such things as thus ever happen and then disappear as fast ... And without such notice as they had appeared before? ...

o   But if such events did happen and in such order ... If one could count on such a thing as order... Then how? ... And more to a point ... What reason? ...

o   Oh well ... Such questions will have been answered by one simple look and gesture brought forth by the inner thoughts and workings of the mind ... Which, without impulse ... Spells its own "Truth" to satisfy the yearn to know ... Without proper response from the recipient of the question asked...

o   THE END

➢ Hearing Aide

o   In the presence of evil ... I see only you ... There has to be more ... If only it's true ... The story books have told me ... That there would be a day ... That only one of us ... Would care to walk away ... The sights and sounds ... I feel within my soul ... Cannot contend ... To the furry of the bowl ... Spinning ... Round and round ... My eyes they cannot stop ... All I ask of this day ... Is for them to pop ... Then they might ... Be halted fast ... or very quickly stopped ... Because now my dear ... I cannot see ... I can only hear! ...

➢ Hello My Friend

HELLO, HOW ARE YOU MY FREND?

○   ... Too much ... Is never enough ... With the struggle almost done ... Those that have not tasted the cold steel of the blade ... Braced for the final blows they wouldst receive this Day ... Though knowing full well they were doomed from the beginning ... Still they fought ... One by one ... Like insignificant ants ... They were picked off ... The day has been sought and conquered by the one so proclaimed as "Him" ... And as the day finishes with a blood soaked sunset off in the distance ... The people ... Of the beam of dark spots that burn their shadows in the light of the clouds of yore ... Rejoice in a revelation that they can now safely go back to their pity-full lives ... Of cower and self-ridicule ... That which hath past is only a memory in the minds of those that could not see the truth of the matter at hand ... That such truth cannot be seen at all ... Unless the ways about the matter are realized in the present ... And reality suggests that they be of factual significance to be used to represent the truth in any fashion or sense! ...

[PAGE INTENTIONALLY LEFT BLANK]

Monkey.–
Knife.–
Fight.!

(. 10 .)

THISLOGUE (*THUR*)

"Wa-wa-wa-wa-wa, meow-meow-meow … Wa-wa-wa-wa-wa, meow-meow-meow! … Wa-wa-wa-wa-wa, meow-meow-meow-meow-meow … Wa-wa-wa-wa-wa, meow-meow-meow … Click" "That's enough of that." Said Ducky, as he turns off the hit TV series, *Hairballs Of The Wild West*, during the main fight scene where Mittens The Kitten, is trying to escape back to his scratching post after robbing the local bar, *The Saucer*, when he is headed off by Felix, the town sheriff. It's an epic tale of the kittens of ye olde west.

[That's ye olde English for the old west]

"Hey Al, wake up, you have missed two days of work and your boss called wondering where you have been. I told him that you were out sick and couldn't make it into work 'till at least Monday. So you're safe, but you really need to get up and start moving around. You're starting to worry me." Ducky said as he poked me trying to wake me from my virtual coma on the couch. "W-where am I? … What time is it, what day is it?" I said to Ducky as I got up from the couch. "It's half past Friday bro." Said Ducky, "You passed out on the couch; I came home the other day from work, and took a relaxing bath. I had my head phones in, and was really enjoying a good bathe. I lost track of time, and when I came out a few hours later, you were fast asleep on the couch. I tried poking you then, but you wouldn't wake up."

"I was wondering where you had gone to, I thought something happened to you!" I stated. "Nah, but why would you think something happened to me?" Ducky questioned. "Well, when I went to pick you up on Wednesday, you weren't at work, and Miko said you might have gone south, and when I came back there was an extra bird hanging in the window; and Miko has always looked at you weird. I don't know man, there have been far too many cases, you know?!?" I said frustrated-ly. "I guess, but nah, Miko looks at all her employees that way. Besides, I'm Ducky, aint nobody gonna quack with Ducky!" He said as he raised his wings and made a pose as if he was showing off his muscles in front of a mirror. I chuckled and said, "Okay Ducky, okay, well I'm just glad everything is fine, and that you're safe!"

"So, what's on the agenda for today?" I asked. "I have a date with that girl from the bar; I think we really hit it off the other day. What are your plans?" Ducky asked. "I think I have something planned, but as of yet, I'm not too sure what. I was gonna see what that one girl from the other day wanted to do. But I think she is busy with her own life, so far I don't really have anyone, or anything to do." I stated. *[Sad face]* "Well," Ducky rebutted, "I am sure something will turn up, maybe you could go for a walk, get some fresh air. You have been asleep on the couch the past couple of days." "Okay, I think I will." I stated as I got up and made my way into the bathroom so I could freshen up and get ready for my venture out on this Friday of nights. "Good bye Ducky, have a good night." I called out to Ducky as he was leaving out the front door on his way to pick up his girl while; I stepped into the shower.

After my shower, I got dressed and headed out myself. I walked down the street and was greeted by a few people as they passed me on their way up the street. I was on my way to the *Bars and Clubs District*. "I'm just looking for a good time!" I stated to myself aloud as I continued walking down the road till I reached the club.

Once inside, I saw many different types of people and many different ways they were mingling, or otherwise interacting with each other. I walked up to the bar and ordered myself a drink and decided to take a seat while I waited. I scoped around and saw a few prospects looking my direction, but I decided to pass on the gesture for the time being. I was on the hunt; I just didn't know what I was hunting for exactly. Not till she came in through the door. *[Excited face]* I was floored from just the sight of her, Tall, but not too tall, with a nice body; very proportionate, and such a radiant smile!

She came up to me and said, "Hi, I'm new to the area." "Hello, it's nice to meet you, where did you move from?" I questioned. "Up north, but it's too cold there this time of year, so I migrated south. I kinda like it here; but what I would like more, is someone to show me around a little bit." She contested. *[Pouty face]* "Well, look no further, I've lived here for a while and would gladly show you around sometime, if you would like." I stated. "That would be lovely." She whispered into my ear as she leaned closer. *[Excited faces all around]*

As she kept whispering into my ear, she was saying all these wonderful things of what we could do, or where we could go. I was getting quite excited at the notion of the woman being so close to me, and talking to me in such a way as to make me forget where I am; even who I am. I stopped her shortly after, and mentioned that we should probably head out and start to explore the town tonight. "Let's not make haste; there is much to see, and much to do!" I stated as I got out of my seat and grabbed her hand.

She quickly polished off her drink and followed me out the door of the bar, and down the street we went. We arrived at my place later in the early hours of the morning; after running around town doing fun things that I will not bore you with here. But suffice it to say that we did some very vigorous acts, very vigorous, indeed! I think we had barely enough energy left to get home and fall asleep on my bed, let alone do anything more on it...

There was a nudge at my shoulder, and the tone of her voice at my ear, "Get up, get up, the show is almost over and you have missed the best parts!" Said Terri, "I don't want you sleeping through the entire performance, and then we are stuck waiting in line to go home; now get up and go get me some popcorn and wine!" "Yes dear." I said, as I got up from my seat to head to the concession to get some snacks. "Did you want white or red this time?" "Ugh, do I have to constantly remind you? ... Red of course!" She said irritatedly.

"Yes dear, I will be back as soon as I can; I just hope the traffic is thin at this hour." I stated as I made my way to the aisle. I headed up to the back of the auditorium and found the concession, there was a short line, so I thought that a small bathroom break would be just what I needed. Since I can't remember the last time I went.

Upon finishing my bathroom adventure, I went back to the concession and ordered two hot dogs, a bottle of red wine, some popcorn, and a soda. The clerk ran me up and gave me the goods before I headed back to my seat. "David, did you get the wine like I asked?" Terri questioned. "Yes dear, I brought you a bottle of it so that I won't have to make you wait quite as long the next time you feel like enjoying a glass." I retorted. As it turns out, the performance was only half over, and as I paid more attention to what was going on; I started to really enjoy the show.

There were acrobats, and people on stilts, there was even a few clowns and some mimes doing 'guilts.' *[That's where you act like a mime, but you have to trip people to make a living at it]* I believe they even staged a performance of some famous playwright or two.

I looked a little harder at the performers trying to figure out what each one was doing, and then I began to notice something odd, something strange a foot. The stage was rather transparent in places, while in others it was more opaque. I was having a hard time figuring out what the deal was. "Hey Hunny, do you notice the stage and how it looks quite odd?" I questioned Terri.

"No, the stage seems just fine to me, why?" She questioned back. "Well, I can't quite put my finger on it, but there seems to be places where the stage gets more transparent; while in other places there seems to not be much transparency at all. No, more like an opaqueness about the floor that is not like any place else I have seen." I stated in a puzzled tone.

"Well there doesn't seem like anyone on stage has a problem with what's beneath their feet, maybe you're just over analyzing things, and this is all just a figment of your imagination?" Terri stated questionably, as if to both reassure me, and judge me at the same time. I shot her a look that conveyed both understanding and caution; I was on to her game!

"No, I think there's something to that floor, and I will find out what is going on!" I exclaimed to her, "I just need to get a better look." "Well, be careful and don't do anything that would get yourself in trouble, I will not bail you out of jail again!" Terri said jokingly, except for that last part, I think. I never could tell when she was being serious or joking around.

Nevertheless, I got up from my seat and walked down the aisle to get a closer look; and what I saw put me in both shock and awe. The entire stage was covered in a clear glass type material to where you could see under the stage in certain areas. It looked rather neat, but what was even neater was that as you stepped back, the parts that were opaque, that you could not see below the stage, spelled out words. The actors were dancing, singing, and performing on the stage; but the stage, in essence was made up of various letters and words. I was taken aback by this and did not really have anything I could say as to what I was witness to. I headed back to my seat and told Terri that I found out something interesting, but that she would have to wait till we got home for me to tell her. "Really? Tell me what you saw." She said. "Yes, but you will have you wait, it's a surprise." I replied.

We got home that evening, after the play and got ready for bed. I made myself a late night snack before brushing my teeth and taking a shower. Terri took one first before she headed into the bed room. I followed in after my shower. "I had a great time tonight." I said. "I did as well, but I just can't help to wonder, what did you find out when you walked down to the stage?" She questioned. "Well," I said, "You could see pretty far down, and there were many people down stairs pulling ropes and wires, and talking into headsets, it was quite busy." "Really?" She questioned, "But you stated that you had something else you wanted to tell me, but you said it had to wait till we got home. So what was it that you wanted to say?" "Well," I said, holding the book from tonight's performance, "This entire thing was all just a 'play' on words!"

And with that, I bid her good night, turned over, and fell asleep...

...THE END...

[PAGE INTENTIONALLY LEFT BLANK]

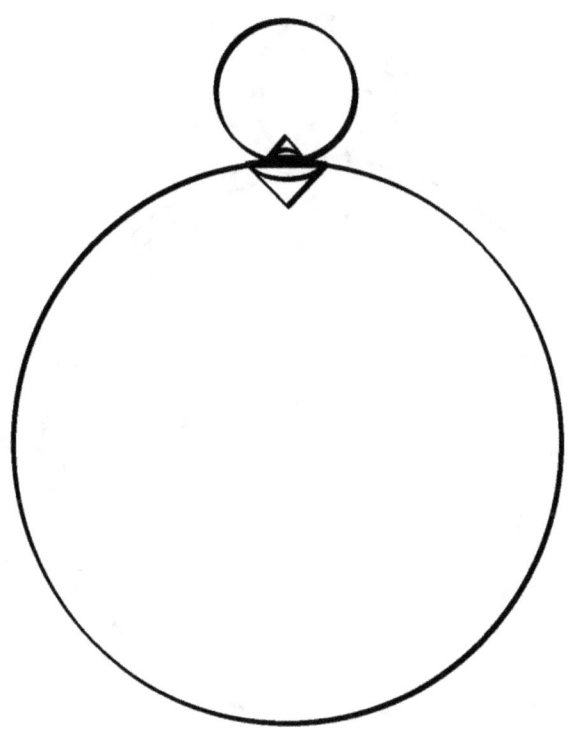

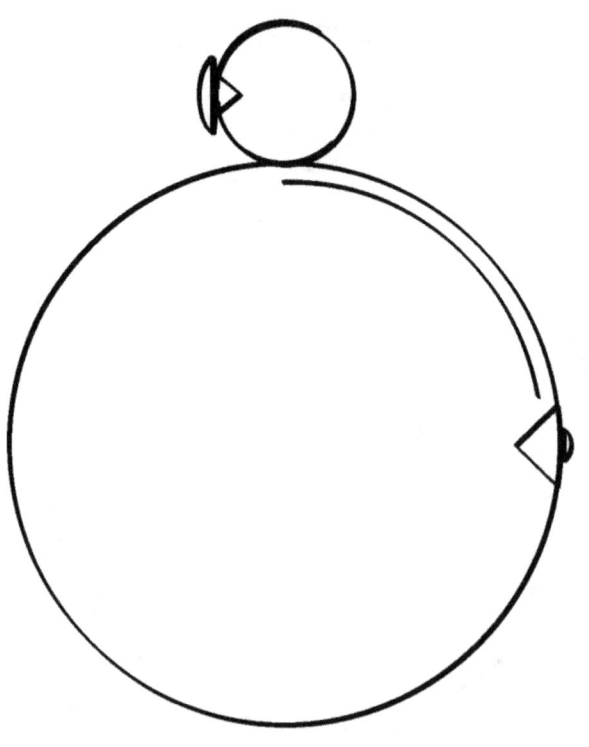

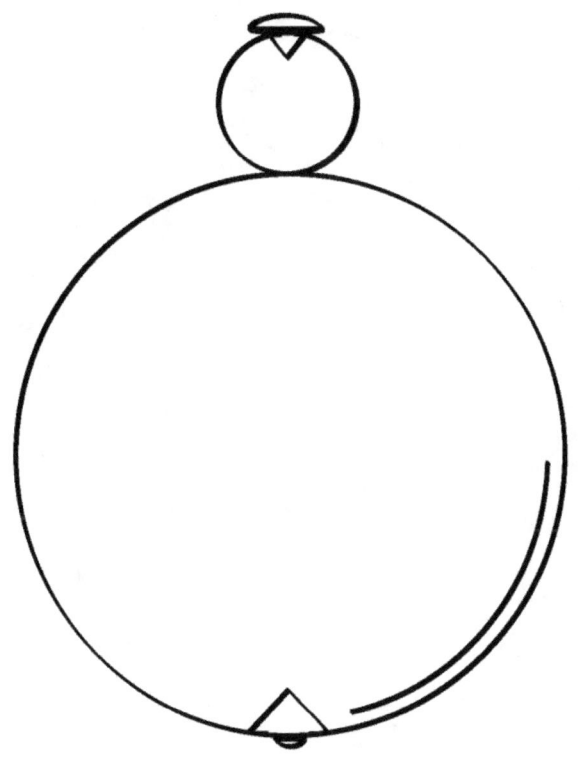

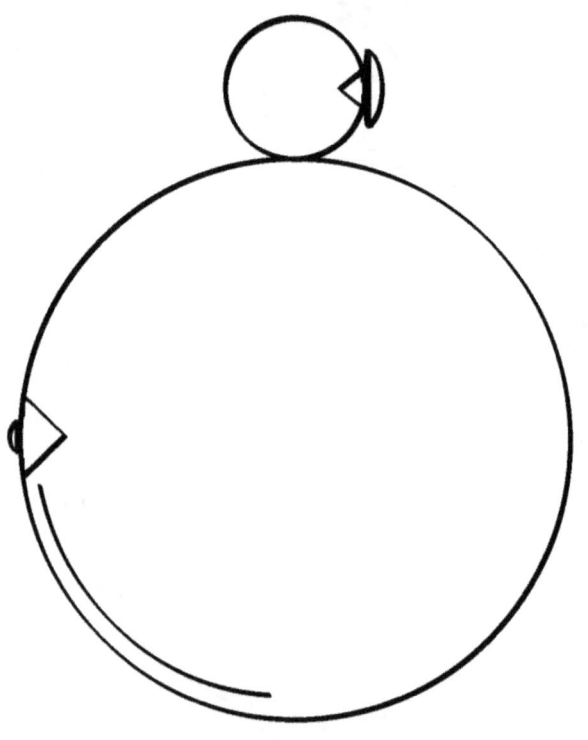

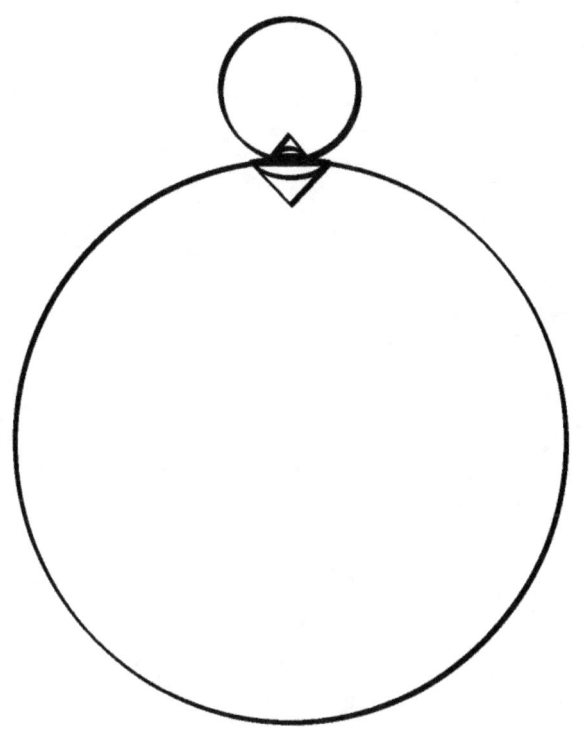

Where's Waldo?

...?

... ...?

... ...?

"Right Where You Left Him!"
(:11:)

➢ Timmy, did you wash the dishes this morning? "No mum, I forgot. Is something wrong?" No, no Timmy, just your father is coming home soon, and I don't want him to see that you haven't done your chores like I had asked you to, two weeks ago. "Awe mum, I shall be right on the matter as soon as the toons are done and finished with." Um, Timmy ... Tim, that is not what I asked you. Now Timmy, if those dishes aren't finished by the time I get back from the back room, you're going to get the beating again. Do you understand? "Aye mum, I got the news." Right, off you go then ... Mr. T-Willigers, are you ok? "Tommy, how can you think of pudding at this

179

time, my head has been bludgeoned by Johnny, from down the street, do you not remember?" Oh yeah, I bet him eleven dollars that he couldn't blind-side you with his mallet without killing you. "Oh did you now?" Uh, that is correct sir. "Well, I cannot get mad at you for telling the truth, my dear boy. Come here, have a lolly." Why thank you Mr. T-Willigers. "Don't mention it." ...

➢ In the time before that which is so prim and proper in the days of yore ... The evil of which there is no other ... Hath reigned for so long ... And with such strength ... That none before the one ... Could have taken so close a grip ... Into the threshold of its realm...

➢ Hickory, Dickory, Doc

○   It's just past three o'clock ... I drank all that I could ... But the Jack is just no good ... Jack is my best friend you know ... There he is where ever I go ... Me and Jack have been through a lot ... But no matter what has happened ... Me and Jack ... We never fought ... Thinking back on what my life has been ... I realize all I have done ... Is create havoc and enact Sin ... Sure ... There have been times of good ... But somehow I feel there never should ... I have been there a couple times ... Where the knife looked good ... I wondered whether I should ... In the back of my mind ... I was thinking yes ... Who would care? ... I do not know ... I wondered ... I cannot think of anyone ... That would wonder about me ... No one that I could see ... But then my friend Jack was in the crowd ... Yelling my name ... He has always got my back I thought ... So I chose life ... I thought why not? ... Hmm ... I wonder how long it would take for the cops to find my body and give a positive ID ... If I drive out to some rural area somewhere ... And mutilate my body ... Before crashing into some tree ... And making it fall into some canyon somewhere ... Just food for thought ... But do I dare? ...

➢ If I were to dye right now ... Would you stand there like a cow? ... Waiting yourself ... Just to dye ... Or would you instinctively learn to fly? ...

➢ What do you think of me ... What kind of person could I be? ... To think such things would be insane ... Unstable ... Or wrong? ... Maybe ... But by whose standards? ... And what law? ... or does law come into play at such a level? ...

➢ Stability is a luxury ... Sanity is a farce of one's own reality ... Reality is in itself ... A figment of the imagination which ... In itself is an unreal aspect of what is perceived as life itself ... Intelligence ... In a society is un-intelligible ... Agreement of such statements or opinions is un-needed ... Nor is it cared about ... But thank you for taking the time to fill out the feedback report ... Your response is greatly appreciated ... No matter how little it is actually cared for ... Or about...

➢ Hills

o   The time was set by the afternoon wind ... The hint of death in the air sent a chill down the spines of those not yet ready to face the force of him ... That hath set the boundaries as thus ... Atop the hill yonder! ...

➢ Eat with the spoon ... Soon-soon ... The moon of June will be upon us ... With the fury of most imminent passion ... One day ... They will arise and conquer again ... With such unbelievable might and chaos ... That the world has never seen before ... Only then can the monkeys team up with the penguins of evil light ... That speaks forth within the shadows of the fallen few ... That defend the spots of pain and suffrage before us all ... I call to thee ... Who beckon me to kill the visions within me that give me strength ... I see the images before me call to me ... And scream as they are slaughtered one by one ... As they watch each one before them being burned and brutally mutated ... As if it were some sick game ... The stench of evil is strong within ... The smell of burned flesh ... All around me makes me happy ... To dye again ... To bring my life to an end ... Would do too easy of an end to my plight ... I need to take one with me ... But I must be choosy of my selection! ...

➢ Land of time was merely a crime set upon the hill thus yonder ... We speak ... And to be spoken of is what I love ... The sawdust of dawn ... Speaks with ease to please the trees of the hill top yonder ... Now we look ... And are witness to the New Year's born again ... As once was thought ... To be a joyous occasion ... Has vastly been understated ... And tossed about to be in the sky ... Blown to pieces and thus admired as such! ...

➢ In the land that so few speak of there is a man ... He is said to be the undead ... And there he must stay ... The land he surveys up to these days ... Is unshifting like the sands that there was always to be ... In his hands he holds a map ... The story goes that those that know of such writings ... In the palms of the hands of the undead man ... Shall be untold but known to be upheld of the golden rules ... Such speech is to be unheard ... But ever known ... Except by word! ...

➢ Tick tock ... Words of the clock ... Go dead at last ... As the seconds past ... I wonder ... As I ponder on ... How could this waiting take so long ... It moves forward ... As I move back ... One less second ... Is on the track ... Rules are there ... To keep me sane ... But the visions I see ... Only harm the brain ... If they speak ... Into my head ... Once again I feel ... I am dead ... Two more tracks down ... And one more to shed! ...

➢ In the middle of the night ... There was a fight ... The season ... For the reason ... To be a sneezing ... I ask you to understand ... That you can't make the plan ... To be in the star light ... With Stan the man! ... In the beginning ... There was one ... The only guy ... To be in the sun ... He stood there looking ... On and on ... But not for too long ... I know by now ... You can't compose

... But I suppose ... You stick up your nose ... At the clouds up in the sky ... And then you swing on by ... The store ... There it sits ... A suit that fits ... Or begs to be in the crowd again ... Orange is like yellow due ... An apple causes bright big hue ... One plus one ... Plus three makes blue ... If you tell this to many ... And hit the floor with few ... Then you might be in the clue ... I rhyme with ... The brightest stories ... I can come up with ... In my dimly lit head ... I block off the latter ... Because I can only see dead ... If this career ... Is all that my mind does see ... Then there is no hope ... For humanity! ...

➢ One of one ... And two of E ... No one likes you ... But there's no one like me ... You must look behind ... The box of your own ... Look inside ... And try to hone ... Try the angle ... Of the inside child ... The box that holds the wild ... If you picture the visions you hold ... You must read and be bold ... To hold the destiny of your own demise ... And learn the phrase that ends with ... "Would you also like fries?" ...

➢ In the beginning I saw the sign ... And it opened up my eyes ... Only after that ... Did I really see ... That my next gig ... Was at the emergency room ... Where I met her ... Her name was Vanessa ... Challenged was she ... But a challenge she was determined to win ... And first prize was her very own car! ... Sadly though ... The prize was not hers to have ... You see ... There was this one guy who gave me some magic beans ... And to the sand ... And the shallows I did throw them ... I pulled out my 45 pistol ... And rested it against the man's throat ... "Give me all your money and ham, or the doll gets it!" I screamed into the deaf man's ear sitting next to me ... What I received was nothing short of a pair of soiled pants ... And two peanuts of remarkable cleanliness for such drastically dirty conditions that I have found myself ... But no ham ... You see ... All this started some sum-

mers ago back on the ranch ... Me and my friends were
out playing in the pasture ... And then we saw a rumble
in the sky ... There was not a sound in the air ... But
merely a rumble or sorts ... You know the kind ... Where
there is a roll to the clouds ... Only ... There were no
clouds ... And we thought the sky was falling ... So we
raised our hands to meet it ... And help it back upon its
feet ... Sadly though my friend "Timmy" *[He liked to be
called Ronda]*, was crushed by a passing train not but
earlier in the day ... And we were a man short for our
tether ball game ... You can't very well decide to play
solo on such games ... Since they are labeled for two or
more ... But I degrease the pan with butter ... Because I
don't trust you to do it ... Besides ... You're not as tasty
when heated to 350°F ... But what do I know? ... I only
have a degree or two *[That lets me know what temperature it is in relation to the ambient temperature of the
surrounding air]* ... Now that you're paying attention ...
Let's begin the story I've been waiting to tell you since
you first turned the cover ... I was there that day ... It
was cold ... How cold, you ask? Well if you were there
... Then you would know ... So save all your questions
till the end! ...

  ➤ In this crazy life that is ... Was ... And will be ...
There was a man in a yellow hat ... A kid at that ... But
none the less, a pro! ... He searched the seas that ever
bees ... For he searched there high and low ... Counting
his travels, was the crow he kept ... And counting them
indeed! ... Unto the night I see the story I seek ... To eat
the worm and speak of the travels hence...

  ➤ Walking down a dimly lighted alley way ... You
notice a street lamp casting light upon the empty street ...
Along the edge there ... You see a three-shelf iron shelv-
ing unit ... On top there is but a glass box, with a sticker
as a latch ... Ominous looking black smoke cycling inside ... Waiting to be released ... Upon closer inspection

... Cracks are noticed on the glass ... Tiny leaks of smoke escape from time to time ... Shifting attention to the other side of the light ... There is a brick wall that extends onward for what seems like forever in both directions ... But again ... Closer inspection, and there is a crack noticed in the wall ... Rather large for what it is ... Ominous deep darkness is felt upon the area just beyond the crack in the wall ... A rush of air flows from within the blackness and the lamp is still on ... But the light on the street goes out as if to be absorbed ... Two glowing eyes are seen off in the expansive distance of the crack in the wall ... And a wicked smile forms ... While ominous laughter is heard ... But from nowhere ... Then everything goes black ... Moments later the lights come back on ... You are on your butt ... Leaned against the wall as the crack has appeared to have sealed itself up... The glass box is still whole too ... The sticker now resembles a crude "Happy face" with a runny black smile and eyes ... As if the "Paint" is still wet ... You look around and figure that nothing has changed ... And nothing has ... For now! ...

➢ Inside

o   The easiest way to ease the pain is just to relax, refrain, and silence the mind to control the brain. Inside every man, there is a boy without a plan, if you find the child inside; give him a kick and enjoy the ride. Rhyming is a passion without action to speak of, you find a word that fits in the story; some of it is fanciful but most of it is boring. No one to hear you cry inside; then you find everyone knows and there is nowhere to hide...

➢ Introtopergalence

o   Chocolaty delight-ness, wondermint of few relent. I ask you, as I ask myself. When will the troublesome delights within my mind end? When will the counter send the time, to be the time, to wing from the courteous challenges from within the floor? I look upon the reflection in the wall, as I contemplate my fate, and stare into the darkness I speak of, leak of, and reek of. I wonder now as I have before. If I kill it, it will restore. The power plant has backups too, but you don't go for that which is taboo. You go right for the source, and of course, it is already flooded with death. Under your breath, you speak of the insanity you witnessed but hours before; as you exited the door to the Promised Land, with milk and cookies in your hand. You looked at the animal crackers in disbelief, as to strife away from the pain. I speak up soon to be inside your brain. Inches I move, and to no relent, I bent the cards in front of your face, and then you spoke; and said the words I was hoping to hear. Till this day I thought you hated me, but now I know you only hated what I am; and so I look at you, and I speak with but one breath unto your face. As I relieve myself of my life with the strife, and kife, of the butter knife within your hands. You don't seem to get what I just said, so you demand, another chorus of just representation; but I can't hear you, for my ears have been cut, and the cords of my brain seared by the pain I speak of; that you caused of me by your vision of such occurrences, that none shall have, nor shall again witness! ...

➢ You wanna see what is going on inside my mind? Step on in ... Don't look behind ... You pass a book shelf on the wall in front ... You step to your left ... Watch out there are dragons a foot ... To your right there are pictures there ... There are mirrors aside ... But you can't see me ... You can't see you ... You can only see what I want you to ... Can you believe that you are here? ... Reading what I have written? ... Can you still understand, that what I have thought, you understand? ... You can't simply see the window without the glass ... You can't simply see the doorway without the way ... Can you really forge a plot in this town you live in ... That accessibly assures that you can escape your own existence ... To the point that you can find solace in the fact that you are forever a slave to your own reality? ... There are only five senses that are known to the race we call human ... There are the simple ones that allow us to explore the world as we see it ... There are the many possibilities that these are all there is to reality ... There are the possibilities that there is nothing outside oneself ... That the reality that there is witness to ... Is the only thing there is ... And the occurrences of physical contact are merely a game played upon ourselves by ourselves to satisfy a yearning to not exist alone ... But if that were the case, how could we tell? ... We cannot ... There is no proof ... And there can't be proof due to the fact that one can't prove a nonexistence! ... The fact that you can't prove a negative bares to the fact that the existences of nonexistence must exist ... Or does that bare to the fact that there is no existence? ... Or does that leave open the conversation that there could be a way to measure the reality of an individual ... Or multiple individuals in a respect that is universal? ... Or does personal preference come in to play? ... Does the perception of a said individual cause a delineation to the measurable outcome of significance? ... Does there mean that any outcome could be possible? ... And that there is no true reality to speak of? ... That the perceptions witnessed by each person ... If they are separate from others ... Is in affect a different concept of reality? ... And that the reality of each person ... Given that they are a separate entity ... Is indeed a separate concept to be explored by each in their own respect? ... True that each person views the existence in their own light ... At their own space ... In their own way ... And that even occupying the same space ... At the same time ... One would see an entirely different outcome of existence ... For a given interval of time ... Two spaces can't be occupied at the exact moment at the exact time ... By more than one individual ... And even in such occurrence ... The notions ... Actions ... Thoughts ... And views of the person ... In particular ... Would come into play to skew the reality of each ... To the point that the reality of each would occur at a completely different aspect of planar existence ... There can never be a unified theorem of one reality ... And there can never be a singular existence ... But what is there to be called to the fact that no one can say they are separate from another? ...

➤ Orange faced ... I feel the disgrace ... The pain you shoot ... From your needle ... Housed deep in your boot ... I only wonder ... What was with the suit ... The glasses made you look for real ... And I thought there was a deal ... The tires you rode in on so fast ... Were not almost dead ... They were just past ... The due date ... Printed on the wrapper ... Was to decide when to throw it in the crapper! ...

➤ The newspaper I use in the room of rest ... The best part of the name at best ... Is that it fits the given name of the room ... For you see ... When I have to square my boom ... I must use some sort of caper ... So I gather a much more boring of paper ... I would get a quilted one ... But instead of sewing together ... What I will just as hastily throw away ... I can gather pre consumer ... And turn it to 100% post ... My way ... Recycling is fun ... If you know how to get it done! ...

➤ In the center are spies ... Like me ... They look upon your flesh ... And at rest ... You notice ... Nothing ... As they want you to ... But I see them ... For what they are ... Just like me ... They live far ... From within your soul ... To outside your door ... They are there ... But nevermore ... The further you push ... the closer they come ... Faster ... Like the beats of their drum ... I hear your heart ... It beats for me ... But never like ... It used to be ... I cannot focus on the past ... For at last ... I see it all ... The numbers call ... To me from on the wall ... They speak my language ... And then I fall ... The time to win ... Is long past due ... But never can ... I win with you ... You will always be ... Just past my reach ... Even with extended arms ... A halted screech ... Pain ... And bewilderment ... Are all I feel ... I cannot stop ... These visions I steal ... To look into your eyes ... As long as I do ... All I see is the color ... And the hue ... It is what best ... Fits for you ... Words of wisdom ... Speak only to the wise ... But they are of the very simplest of disguise! ...

> Liefe

o   In the middle of the night, they got to win the fight. I ask you now, can anyone say to thee that what has past into the night was not a horrific beast, but none which one said true to the cause of those not yet understood to the situation at hand? If you think you can pass into the flame of man to which there is no end in sight, then you shall be burned and cast into never ending sorrow and demise that causes one to rethink the situational unspeakable. Orange, blue, one, and two; if you sit on me, I will **** you! The time is hear and gong, now is the reason for the season at hand; if you ask the clowns to stop, and then you pop a pill of courage, Stan the man will eat your head, and out will come the cheese ... On the hills of pain, there was lain, a man of responsible reasoning; to be held accountable of the burning nature of the cows in the valley. If you look upon the visions in the sky, as they all float on by, you should see what I have in hand for you my son. A play on words is like a flight of birds. If you look them in the eye, run for cover as they die, vehicles are fun to drive when you can handle yourself for a time, when you drive one into a crime, you can make it possible, to make it plausible; to be in the lime light you see ... But would you do this for me? ...

> One day I was walking along the road and there were two angles in front of me, one said come my son, let me help you; the other simply said *[With a demonic*

voice] Die! And as they both looked upon my figure, I began to feel urges inside me saying no to one, and yes to both. And as those two visions vanished into the light of day I looked away, for not to see them again; only problem was, that they were never really gone. Just unnoticeable to my eyes. All along, and forever more I heard that voice of hers say: come with me my son I will protect you, while the other simply, and encouragingly, still says "Die!" ...

➤ Two eyes go blind, as the world is filled with questions. Now life is ready to settle the score! ...

➤ Mind Catch

o   Well I think right now *[Though not to be rude]*; your handwriting is pretty bad itself. But it's ok I'm sure things with work out in the end ... All you have to do is understand, that you can't change what's happening around you. You can only realize it controls, and stimulates, you in ways that cause you to believe you're in control. The mind functions, in ****** up ways ... Ways that cause one to daze the days away. Food for thought, or maybe not ... It's up to you, what you do ... Maybe you should take up Kung Fu. Or Thai-Chi of sorts, some consider it a sport. Though you don't have to retort, but be wise of the disguise. The one you seek will soon surmise; that you're not yourself within your mind. Watch out behind you, or you'll go blind! ...

➤ Then there was a man that had the plan to be the one in the sun, but he had the smallest gun in the west; but it was also the best, because he passed all the tests there were, to be heard by the birds of the south, but it was not by mouth. But were there ninjas in the air? ...

➤ Oak

o   I take this time as a literary escapee ... I rhyme these words so they do not rape me. 1 plus 1 plus 1 makes 3 ... If you ask again I will hit thee ... And you know what I mean the mostest, it is the possible coast to coastest ... I do not understand my own voice, I do not know what other choice ... I may, or may not, be the best. But I will pass your test! ... Please read every third word ... Don't skip around, 'till you see the bird ... I ask you now, and then I ask you then ... What has your respect, except the hen? ... I say to thee, and I say to you. What are you gonna do? ... You wonder, and wander, into the tree, but you don't even say yippee! ...

➢ Oops

○ "Taste the tiny squirrels. Chocolate is their nature. Wonderfully yummy is the day that starts with danger. Do you think that my name makes me fat? I should dye with the magical cat? Should I eat that?" ...

➢ Pepsee

○ A Pepsee, one or none, "That is all I ever wanted." To be the light, not far from the beam of dark spots, in the mind of those delusions that perceive to be told as fact.

○ Awe, the time to think is through, now is the time to act without the distraction of the mind; for as the world turns, the insanity within it grows to an over whelming sense of madness, and inner turmoil to which those already dead; or have managed to shut the "Working" side of the beam off, can finally breath without seeing the clowns.

○ Those "Happy" clowns, that tend to appear without warning, and always haunt you with their "Balloon animals" and "Carnie-tricks." But the True evil is the mime, for the mind of the mime is one that can destroy one's own freedom to think, but about all but nothing at all! ...

➢ Such radical acts of turmoil and chaos have ended such a start of things as a beautiful development. I have done something I fear, I can never repay, such debts that have been caused by my stupidity and inner rage. But hey, life as they say is nothing but a box of chocolates. I don't like raspberry filling or that weird toffee-like crap. The nuts of life are good; I'm one of them I fear. Ha-ha-ha … Hey, it's all good; I'm not crazy, just very complicated, and confused at times! …

➤ In the beginning, there was one. And he said there be it; the shining stone I shall make all of everything from. And to this day, there were none other than said stone and those be gotten thereof. And I say to thee, "Let there be light, and let that light be good." For I say it so, and so I say it, and there I see that there is good light and the light I see that is there, is for now, and for always, good for I have seen and say it so; but then not in the other realm from whence I was, but never was afore from. And from said place there be another of such beings as to cause similar effects to occur in the same manner as I have simplified with wordage. But again with the acts of which is upon us this day. I see the occurrence of unspeakable trials and tribulations as to cause the entire change of existence to be spoken only through acts to be forgotten this day, and for all days for there is no end in sight of the carnage and chaos to be had in this realm of consciousness…

➤ It was the best of times, it was the worst of times … To my right was my musket, to my left my weasel. I, and again, I shall fight for the rights to bear arms. Yes, this is the day of days as I sit atop the hill again and ponder what sort of stain I shall create, but wait, I cannot do such things with so much to live for as a little voice beneath all the neglect rings out inside my head. And so I stop and question my intent as if the voice I heard means anything to me. I sit down though, as if to understand what I think I thought I heard. But alas, it is again upon me, and I hear the voice again. Only this time angry, loud and very much real as it speaks to me about taking care of myself, and taking the time to listen now, and again. But I cannot see from the point of view of my mind. It has all the thinking to itself, while I am left with the leftover thoughts that were too rich; or otherwise too clouded with mixed fillings of guilt and self-righteousness, and pity. I say there beagle man, toss me a beagle! I need the nourishment to fulfill the needs of everyone I see, and therefore speak to, about the crimes I see in my daily life. The injustice paid to the flapper of the garbage receptacle is done so in vain due to the neglect of the can itself to sympathize. "How do I drive a bike backward when I cannot even pedal it forward?" I ask myself as I sit in my car waiting for the motor to turn on, I have sensually talked to it, and rubbed it in all the right places, but still it sits there coldly weighting on its tires, as I sit inside it all stressed out, and panicking that I am going to be late and its only five-thirty. I wake up every day, have the same breakfasts made the same way, and I go to work and drive the same root. I even wear, sometimes, the same suit. But when I awoke this fine summer's day, I, instead, of toast, drank a glass of whine. I took a right around the coast, I even made the company weenie roast ... But when I went to bed, I did not arise. Perhaps I should have drunk the rye instead of the chardonnay. This day...

➢ I say there Jim ... I know your name isn't Jim *[Unless it is]*, but Jim, do you see what I see? Is that there a yellow wood? Or perhaps a piss stained forest, how could that be? Must I be forced to walk the dainty road that, covered in moss, never stood a chance of being talked to by foot? ...

➢ Into the focus the camera knows. Where did all the fairies and candlestick men go? Where are the lollipops and sugar sticks, and the dreary-dreary pogo ticks? I wonder myself as you wonder now, why did I ever touch the cow? When was the evening to be the one that is down with the movie? And then the cloud hit me right smack dab in the back, I know now what is the attack, there is the time and the place to be, in the shadow of the real PD. I don't understand all the darkness I speak of, nor do I contemplate all that which I see. All I can do is to understand you, and for you to understand me. The bottom line of this garbled recollection of past and pertinent future events; is that I once was a balloon again, and you were the one that popped me my friend. And then there were days I would remember to brush, and then there were days I would forget my lunch, if it weren't tied in a sack and stacked on my back ... I knew there were two things I could do, but I didn't do them, because they were already through...

➢ "So, Robby, what is that on your back son?" I do not know dad, maybe it's the tattoo I got at the fair last Sunday. "Well it sure aint a bug bite, that's for sure!" Well you know what they always say, live and let die. "Yep, you have learned a valuable lesson my deer friend." ...

➢ In the evening, they were coming for me ... And I knew it was game over in the hand basket of *** ... I could see the faces of all those I let down by failing like I have ... And again I look upon the keyboard I bash in confusion ... "Today is a beautiful day to die," says a little, but powerful, voice deep inside my brain ... I look through my eyes to strain to see him staring back at me; with intense conclusions that start to make sense only now ... I scratch myself to understand the pain, but alas I am alone again, deep within myself like I have been, many times before ... Staring into the night as dawn blinds the shadows that come to the beam to kill the visions they cause themselves this day ... But along comes the knight, the shining of the metal flesh he holds into the beam to cover the tracks left behind by his fallen foes of plenty ... The never ending turmoil that is caused to be this day in the light of the few that know the truth, that this has been known all along to be told as false ... But the real story at hand will be in to the darkest day of the light rays that speak to be told as factual recurrences...

➤ Enter the light of the hand of man ... The meeting plan to the God of fire shall be the light behind the man's hand of the lamb of the righteous one that shall be in ... The spark of light shall once again be in the hands of the chosen one ... The feelings passed into the spores of fire ... I sat there with my desire ... To touch you there, but soon there would be perspire, and I thought about what I would ... And then there possibly, if I could...

➤ Showoff

o I see the cat in the celling ... It stares back at me ... I ponder it thinking ... Does it really see ... Is its brain too big, or too small? ... I finally realize, I know nothing ... At all! The fan is a spinning, counting down my doom ... With the setting up so high I feel time will come soon. Stop it does, oh so fast ... I barely have time to focus on the past ... The future skips a generation or two ... So I'm sorry, there is no me and you ... I promised I would be there ... But I didn't know where there would be ... I told you that I might not make it home till just past three ... I guess I lied to you, but this is the last time I swear ... The boat man is waiting, but I have nothing to wear! ...

➤ Speedr

o As the story begins we see our star character standing on the corner at a telephone booth ... Dressed in a trench coat, he looks at his watch and then down the street as if he is waiting, and has been for some time. Time goes on, and still he is there with his brief case in hand. Along came a spider, sat down beside her, ate his cream of wheat ... She looked at that spider sitting beside her, her friend came back from the kitchen, and screamed "Hey, that's my seat!" down chased the spider did the two of them do, and wouldn't you figure, that none of them knew; that the spider was only a distraction of few, to lead them poor girls down the pipes and then sue the plumbers, of that, there is two. For the whey they were going ... "I'm sorry, have we met before?" "Oh, how do you do?" Hmmm, interesting predicament, hey what time is it? I ask you this to get out of that, you answer back, "Chill putty-tat!" But I purr back, that I'm a man, not a cat...

➤ What is there, and what shall be, are two very different things to me. I see his face more clearly now than ever before, I see what he sees, think what he does, do what he was; I will be one day of days, one way of ways, I will once more be in the shadow of the light of evermore, the one that seeks to be the floor, the one that seeks to win the score and forever more be the one of one's of the land, and sky, to be the king of none, to be the one flew by...

➤ Contra-diction, is the piction, for fiction; what are you still reading me for? I said put me on the floor, I want to be one wiht the dorr, and hit oyu on your way out. That way you can't complain when I strain your brain with my complaint of how happy I was, when I had that fine buzz. But now that it's over, I'm older then I was when we started this, all that time ago. But it feels like just a flow down a river with a quiver, a quaver, and soon another favor. Hey can you get me a bud? Someone that can watch the kids as I go out the door, hit the floor, and ask for more. A cycle of fiction, to be that one with the itching to be pitching my truth to you for a flavor to be held. That light looks good, lime was the flavor of the day, you said all the way to the fair, when I gave you that dare that you could not run fast enough to hit that bare; and get away without your hare. But don't worry, I have your hare in a snare, to keep it safe for all time until you die, then it is mine for all time, till I get sick, or pick a stick out of the fire and burn your hair off of your back;

because it's on the attack. Don't worry; I will not snicker, when I snack! ...

Working Titles Don't! ... Or Do They?

("Food For Thought, But I'm Still Hungry, Maybe because I'm Not Thinking; Na, I don't think so")
(:12:)

➤ Staring The Face
  o   In the morning I stand there and stair into the eyes of my doom ... Blue as they reflect my ever wondering mind ... I stand there a moment longer and ponder the unspeakable, the unreachable, the morbidly teachable ... "Why, oh why, did I leave the Oreo cookies there to die?" Is the last question burned within my mind ... A moment longer still and now I am blind ... An organ donor I said I am, but that is before I knew what it was ... I thought I was gonna donate my piano, or perhaps a can-o- ... Beans, maybe ... But baby, you know I still wish you were mine. With my last breath I form your name in the mist ... Crap it's misspelled I think, damn you will be pissed ... When you see it ... My cold,

dead body, a silhouette in space, the crapified look upon my face ... But a smile cracked because I know you can never again hit me with your mace. Thinking back to the path I chose this night, just before that I thought I might ... Just for a fright, I thought I would bite, at the invitation from that colorful sprite. Knowing now what I did not, I should have taken longer on my thought. But took a right step instead of left, now that my mind is lack of cleft, I ask my question within my mind, because that's the only part that remains un-blind...

➢ In the opposite side of the double stick mirror ... I look at you and you look so clear ... Once I see past all these ripples, I will speak unto your ear, let you know that now I have no fear ... I look unto the glass for which the name was such ... And see myself looking at me. "What witch craft is this?" I ponder, and again my reflection ponders with me, almost exactly the same, but with a snare to allow me to wonder if it really is me on the other side, or is it someone else with something to hide!? ...

➢ I see the face within the space within my place that I call my mind ... But not only does he who is me see what I see, he knows who, what, were, and in what clothes, I do pose. For a rose is a rose, but a chameleon can be of any color ... Just like the base you put on your face to hide your real you, like that faint spot over there; mother...

➢ Summer Times
  o Dearest summer, nay to Fall
  o Can the springtime winds recall?
  o I say dear Donna, what's that word?
  o That book about a mocking bird?
  o Has no one the gumption to say
  o Burn the book and throw the cat away? ...

> Summer Love
  o   Summer love is the love of summer times
in the winter rhymes for a spender ... I just come and go,
I just don't know why, I'm here for the show I say; goes
and comes, again and again, and then one more time ...
But when the time is right and the night is as bright as the
sun, I will win again and again, and then I will be the
kind of show, and then you will know what time it is.
But when I say it's time to play, you will again be in the
show to be the one that wins the cash. And then you will
know what I mean by what I say, and then the game will
play away until that faithful day that comes again and
again...

> My thoughts are rambled, hypocrisy is all I see, I
know what the words are, and all I can do is scream out
the answer. But I don't know how to have self-control
when it's not my turn to speak. I know not what I do, I
say things that are not true, and I do what you tell me not
too ... So what is this, is this a joke, and what am I to tell
the pope? I cannot speak and I cannot do, I will not be
there by the moon. I cannot give you what you spoon,
and I will be the alpha crew, in the bushes by the store,
there is a cardboard box ... Bring it swiftly, like a fox! ...

> Time
  o   What time is it here today, what time is it
in the world would you say? Time keeps slipping and I
don't know why, what about you there, that guy; what is
your problem can you not see; there is a bear behind that
tree? What has he got inside his hand, oh it's just Sharr-
man on demand. What a commercial to do, watching a
group of bears take a poo. Boy oh boy, what a sight, I
might as well just watch some picks at night. A cleverer
show about a man and a hat, a cat with a bat, and a suit
that's just flat. Why do these things amuse everyone?
Not one of them is alive anymore, and none of them was
fun. The story today has just flown away, like bees on a

flower, or hands on a tower, time keeps slipping by and by; by the time you read this it's my time to die. I never could get the words to stick; the more I whine the more I am a prick. One and one, and three make two. The time is here, but where are you? I ask this question many times a day, what would you do, what would you say? I don't have answers to things like this; on that same commercial, I think the third bear only took a piss. The paper was wasted only to sell, a used product, but heck, oh well. One less thing to worry about, at least while he is busy, you can make out. The worry that people have is just that, when you see a bear, don't run, just grab a bat. Steal his hat, paper, or cat. They hate those things we do to them, but come on people, it's all phlegm. The reason I say such dastardly things, is the same reason I don't have wings. I mean I could buy them at the store, or restaurant, but I can't handle being on the spot. Saying nice things and catching a breeze, the story here is who is the sleaze? I look around the room and pick out the snot; I check out the scene and decide why not. I should eat here; I have done it before my dear. The one in the back facing the floor, that way I can watch everyone and even the door. Got to be careful when you are like me, someone is always looking so I can't even take a pee. I see their cold eyes staring deeply at me, as I breathe I swallow, the food that I cherish the most; I don't mean to boast, but I love a good roast. As I stare back, I see them ponder, whether they should wonder, I give a gesture back as to see if their intention is to attack. If so I am ready to go, take a blow and make a good show...

       o   Hmm-mmm-mmm, like Mac-Daddy-Donalds; I say damn! Water, like your daughter is hotter than hot, but I decide why not, I will try a taste, not to get burned I cover my base. Cover my face, and go in for the try, make a fly-by and escape like that guy on the news; that stole that car last Sunday, didn't you hear, he apparently got away? Over kill, just like the pill, is chocolaty delicious; but be careful of the amount, because it's quite often vicious. Sleep is over rated, I know your doctor hated you to challenge his authority, but come on chick you can sleep with me. I'm sure when I'm done you'll be tired, and we'll both have fun. I promise to be gentle, kind and cute, but if you're not careful I'll give you the boot. Watch that step, the door is quite rude, and it packs quite pep, when it's in a bad mood! Literary genius, but I'm illiterate, what are you talking about? Man I'm full of it. I cannot see, I must be blind, I could not see past your fine behind! Don't give me your name I aint got no shame all I want is digits, and no, I aint about *******. Oh man, I feel that itch, like a witch in the wind; I cover my shin, fake an ache and prepare for some sin. Hehe I think, as I imagine something pink. What a sight I know, hey baby you want to watch the snow? I got a warm place with a fire, no flame of course, but lots of perspire! My mind is on a roll, I fear I can't control, fear did I say, awe heck, more like no way! I use it for good, but then again I always should, the good of man to have a nice play, to get girls in the can. Some say that is a play of "The man!" …

       o   But at the end of the day, when all the fire is gone, whose there stirring the ashes along, the help is still tending the kill, making the way till he is dead and ill. No one says thanks; no one but the fakes, poking with their rakes and throwing rocks at his shakes. The man only wants to go home to his wife and kids, but at the end of the night when the time is all his, all he can think about are the stories he has seen; the people that were mean, and that toilets he has cleaned. To tell his family of the shame he has shined, would be a mockery of his masculinity, but again he is bold; and the truth must be told, so with head held high on his way home he waves bye to the jerks, sluts, and the works. Home is where the hat is lain, and again and again that is told to the brain; but is it ever thought what makes a hat? Well probably not. It takes workers in a shop, or kids by the pop; toil and turmoil make a hat what it is, have you ever seen a hat made out of Pez? Crack in my back, like a track, I sit on the sack and lay a smack; what are you doing today? Did I hear you say, you would make a trip to the woods? Maybe shop for some goods, how about you do a thing or two; first of all learn how to tie your shoe. Watch the news and learn to lose. The first things first, and that is the worst. What would you do without you good friend Blew? Well I think you would not be able to find her clues, or maybe smack that poor guy with the news, that the show he stars in is not to be viewed, by kids with big shoes. In the morning I lie in my bed, and grab a hold onto my head, I listen to voices within, and wish I were dead, that way I could sleep through my dread; of the laughter and the prodding that is said. The people I see, and the visions before me, haunt like a tree; or a crow that you see, driving in desert, forest, or city. The old man down the street had some meat, he asked you if you would like to share a seat, and help him eat his very large meat. How to say it nicely that you don't want to offend, and then you pretend to accept, and befriend this poor old man; and as you go to shake his old hand, he pulls out a knife and kites you, as you strife toward him, with intent to be kind; you turn your attention to your own behind, the old man was quick, slick and has a trick, or two does he not? Keep your guard up so as not to be caught. The fish in the barrel are dangerous and slick, shoot very carefully, them buggers are quick! ...

➢ Title

o   Inch by inch the knife came down ... And toward the end I saw it ... I walked up to the king, and hit him in ... Now floor it ... I was asked, "But why the day would come?" And in it would be the answer. But nevertheless, were the questions that passed even faster…

➤ Toshey

o The post watchman circles his station in the last stand he will ever face … "The race is on and the charms are gone" … Said the night watchman … To be in the class of glass to be witness to be … That which does not hurt me, makes me stronger even longer in the shadow of the night; I stand there victoriously sending a meaning to the few that less fortunately shine upon our ways these days … The night steels visions from the sun and casts them upon the moon in effort to over shadow the relentlessness of the hours to be cast into unforgiving light, with spots of darkness to cause the missing scenes of brightness in the mind … Lack thereof, the sightings that present themselves in the reality of realism…

➤ Me … Iz … Un … Rhino! …

o In the morning time, I saw the fish standing there, and he called to me, he said "Dear Timmy, come hither into the light." I stood there looking at him and said "My name isn't Timmy." The fish looked at me and continued rambling on and on about his little life that I figured was insignificant at the time. And the more and more I heard him call me that name, T-Timmy, yes that fretfully awful name, *[A name I have grown to loath]*, The closer I came to ending his pathetic little life, or so I thought…

➤ Real monkeys … Of the amazon … Of the amazon … They-say-hey…

o Into the night I hear them calling me. They sit there and chant to the inner side calling me to come hither, but I beckon back at them to wait till the dawn. "Neigh," they say to me, that now is the dawn of which I am to be. Pausing, I'm still pondering the ways I have been thus before, with the wanting of the few less than thou, which hath been to be the one that hath hardened the sword to the point of no return. I cannot turn back now, I have passed into the light not darkened under to which there is no end in sight, save for the death of the one true that hath passed into the light of none. The darkened spots of black light of the one that hath been here, but never was to be in the blood line of the few that are to be, shall notice that the path of good that is to be never, was into the noble hood, that shall bring down the halls of the evil, that lies in wait until the time that is called upon to save the day that has already past...

➢ In the past I have been torn and tattered, beaten and battered, but stood for what I believed in ... I don't ask for much but expect a lot from those I work with. I don't consider them worth the time I spend but I consider the time I spend worthwhile. I understand the things I do as useless, but useful to be fulfilling. The focal point of my life has been to be considered as a motivated, dedicated, but seemingly uneducated individual. I speak with clear thought and concise judgment with the consideration that I only judge those whom are prejudged by the people that present the most impactful outcome of the objective at hand, perhaps then, one could say, I rejudge them ... Or would that just be post humorously stated? Judging is, definitely, overrated! ...

➢ Making of the man shall take weeks, or hours, to be conceived as just and true, the entire construction must be lined and penciled with the right type of glue...

➢ I can see them clear as day, if I close my eyes they disappear, for the moment I am in the clear, I open though to realize, I have just been deceived by my own eyes. Rubbing them makes no sense, only then are they blurry, for the moment, to cause the senses to adjust and then a moment later they are closer than before! ...

➢ No one can hear me as I scream into the glass in my head. No one can see me as I scream into my bed. At least that is what I read, on the wall I see within me. I did not write the words I read, I realized then, those were the words I would bleed...

➤ I sit down for a moment to breathe as I contemplate the occurrences that have past inside of my mind, I suddenly go blind. Then I see myself but from behind. I cannot move, and then I see the horror to be. The visions are true that are inside of me, I wonder a moment longer and see the truth; I see what they wanted all along, and by the end of the song I have hummed, to release the tension inside the walls of my trapped mind, I cannot see myself from behind. All I can see is the inside of me, red with blood my insides are; fresh are the wounds, and soon will be the scar. I cannot change the past events, I cannot change the post relents, to see within, the future presents; the causes to be sent to the superficial place I am to be. I cannot stop the train to let my self-rest without pain ... Inside the walls I keep the unspeakable of what I do not want to see, I have witnessed at least once, but more than I could recall; truth of much, but not of all! ...

➤ Caught between the hole in the wall, and the 8-ball ... I choose the latter to escape this space ... My room is littered with picante de pace ... Running the Marathong ... She scratches her nose ... Wait, wait ... There is just a run in her hoes ... Asking the wall ... For some room to grow ... Move he must ... But don't we all? I cannot stand it ... I really can't do ... All that I live for ... Is because of you ... This ballad of noise, that I just said ... Is for all that air, that fills up my head ... You know I love you ... And I always will ... But do not think of me, when it's your time to kill ... Go-bots, they go ... No-bots, say no ... Hoe-bots ... Well you know ... I think they work for Santa, at least when it's time for "snow!" ...

➤ I call upon you, the damned and broken few ... Those that lye deep inside my soul ... The ones that come to me to die ... Those that run and hide ... The chaos that beckons you to be ... I call on you to now be free ... To bother me no more ... I am not your keeper ... Nor have I kept score ... I close my eyes ... And all I see ... Is that so deep inside me ... Is what you want me to see ... It is nothing ... As if I just blocked out the sun ... And no ... It's hardly as much fun ... You look at me when I look right through what I can see ... But only what I do ... In the field ... I have dreams too ... But when I awake ... I am usually black and blue ... This happens often ... It's not new ... I have accepted my fate as such ... I have asked to stop this ... But have I asked too much? ...

➤ I ask too much of you ... Now I ask what you can do? ... And now you show me the bottom of your shoe ... The reason that I do not leave ... Is because the shoe you wore had a cleave ... The time I take to destroy myself, is more than enough to build that shelf ... The one you asked me too, twice before ... When we saw that expensive one in the store ... But really it was not that much ... I just didn't want to burn that much cash like it were hash ... The time I could have spent to put it together, I told you was shorter than it takes to change the weather ... But sadly I was wrong again ... Like I always am ... And here we are again ... Back to bed for the day is done ... You are my friend, because you have won ... On through the night, we put up the gloves and end this fight ... Till tomorrow comes, and my nerves are back ... Ready and willing to defend your attack...

➤ I eat rice crispy ... Treats from the ground ... Just like huckleberry ... Always hounded by you, I react like I always do ... You never understand how I work ... Just like a jerk ... A creek in my neck ... Irrigating my back ... And front deck ... Perhaps I should just write an owner's manual for you, since you treat me just like a tool...

➤ I write a certain passion ... I ask for a certain action ... I know this is only a fraction ... And your bewildered attraction ... Is only a reaction ... For my satisfaction...

➢ The numbers game ... Is all about fame ... There is no shame ... Unless the gong calls out your name...

➢ I awake to the smell of toast ... Walking down stares ... I notice, at most ... She has no hair ... So I boast ... "As the host, who serves the most ... I must coast, to coast ... Like I were in space ... Or a ghost ... What is that feeling in my chest? It feels tight ... Like there is a pest." Digging deeper with my fist ... Now I am starting to get pissed ... Anger follows, and vessels in my head ... Are pulsing rapidly, I am getting red ... "You would not like me when I get mad" I said ... But just as true, I would not like me when I am dead...

➢ Following in your footsteps would have me reading in your shoes ... I have no idea, why you play the blues ... But when I put your pants on ... And take over your life's work ... Don't sit there mocking me, and calling me a jerk ... You once were suggestive, and supportive of my views ... Now all I see you doing is following those "Me-too's." ...

➢ Mocking me ... From behind my eyes ... I live my life as a disguise ... The painted faces ... That I wear ... Seam all covered by my despair...

➢ My head is spinning ... When I close my eyes ... I am stationary to my surprise ... It is my eyes that move ... And let me see ... That which I hide so deepily ... I do not want to wait anymore ... I think it's time to settle the score ... You read my words like I am some whore ... Jealous of my gift you are ... You always want to ride in my car ... I never argue, I just sit and take it ... You act like I owe you something ... Like a pig in a blanket ... If there is not meat when you bite down ... You will complain to the circus clown ... No matter who was responsible for the meatless bread, you ate instead...

> I cry at night inside my hands, using them as my eyes' bed pans. You look my way, but not at me, as if I am not there, or you can't see. Inside I'm torn, but not apart, there are some fragments that hold together my heart. I try to hold on, I try to be strong, but lost; is this fight inside. Gone with the wind, and low as the tide; is that esteem I called my own. Out of my shell, I finally emerge, and as I thought, you're no longer home...

> Although I have come to a positive time ... I still see my existence as a life of crime ... Punishment must ensue ... But not before I take care of you ... Like El Mer did when he concocted his glue ... The problem with people is, they worry too much ... Like curious Jorge, with his hands on the clutch ... Where were we going, and what will we do? Too bad he had a handle on the tube of super glue ... Now every time he steps ... Or makes a motion to stride ... The car takes a jolt ... Or offers to glide ... The range that I let it ... And the time that it goes ... Is further than even Pinchocio's nose...

> Each side ... Controls the other ... They fight for power, but never shudder ... They always know, the other's weakness ... Never yielding, or showing duress ... The time they take, to patiently plan ... This attack is far at hand ... There is limited time, left on the clock ... This is not merely, just a cake walk! ...

> Looking deep ... I see inside ... But I see two ... There are not many things to say ... There are not many things to do ... There are only voices ... Some of them are you ... Telling me things ... Mostly what to do ... I shy away from what I see ... Hearing color is what I be ... now there are not many, ways to go ... There is only out ... Or down the hole ... The time I spend ... So deep inside ... Is what I used, to flee and hide...

> I hide my disguise ... Deep within my variable meat pies ... I look through the bars at night ... Hoping for a monkey knife fight ... They once were frequent

about the grounds ... Now I fear they have been prey to the hounds ... No one has seen, or heard of them since ... All except one ... By the name of Vince...

➢ Pu-dine

○ Put in a predicament, man that's full of it, what the **** chuck, aint that a piece-o-sh*t? I write without reason, just enough for four seasons; two makes three, so whatcha gonna be? If you look around the room today, don't be scared to stare and say; "Hey there Jonny, what you got for me?" "Is there water under the bridge today?" "Or is there only crackers that pave the way?" Orange and green make purple sheen, the wonders of the world are marvelous; but again they cannot make it past the water of the most unspeakable evil, that hath yet to be spoken for, or dealt with. Yet, it's but he that alone, has the power to unite; and crush all that he surveys before him. I speak of the fallen few that go before us many, that have no name to call upon, but yet surrender our identity as a whole under one name. Judgment for the plaintiff as such, in the order of the spots of light that beckon to be released as they should; into the night of evil light that taunts the shadows within to come and play as any innocent being with such a weakness as such. The only way I have found to truly satisfy the insanity of the puddin' is to eat thyne meat, for how can you have your puddin' if you don't eat your meat? ...

➢ ... I woke up in a catamaran the other day, 'twas night fall; and when it did, it hurt like the dickens. I will tell you right there, that the dickens really knew how to hurt...

➢ ... Fourteen of them were staged at my feet, and two at my arms. I knew I could take them all, I knew I would be victorious if I could only reach my thumbs; if I would only do that one simple act of self-preservation, than I might be able to save others. All too soon I realized that this was an effort lost, and I alone shall suffer the greatest loss...

➤ Yes Tim, I do like to eat cotton candy when I ride the buffalo down Main Street. Why do you ask?

➤ ... Nigh, nary will ye be in the I's of the driver man's daughter whench. She be for me, and me alone, "Arrg," I say, Arrg and arrg too you to! ...

➤ Cause I said so, Bit*h's ... Space, time, and consonance; all good things much count on a pair of 'rents. If you doubt this must be true, how did you come about, I do ask, "Who created you?" Questions to the questionable, the rehearsed answers are encourage-able. But does this mechanized, trivialized, almost satirized, vision of the truth beg to be counted as such, and thus be relied upon to build our fences against the masses that rely on our open gated policy? I speak not for the chosen many, but for the impoverished few that know nothing of the tortures money brings. Why, those without, never have to worry about when to stick their noses straight up into the air to avoid being stared at straight in the eyes by those without! The have-nots are the truly free. Free from prosecution, free from tyranny, free from hardships such as mortgage payments, and food bills. How can they sit there and know these horrors, having to go to bed at night, thinking of the credit mongers, and the banks that wait in their closets at night, hoping they will sleep soon so their blood can be drunk by the morning? Our economy may have created the walking unemployed, but is there a cure? ...

➤ Make it in the pants and we stop a while, the jester makes a smile, and we look at the pile on the ground. One plus one makes 3, before you look at it all and stop a while to listen to the footsteps we be. In the middle of the night, there was a horrific fight that woke the nation in two. One from the east, a sight to say the least, it was a horrific style of beast. The north then came, but this was more the tame. And the answer we all were waiting on. The minute passed and then at last, we heard the gong. They once said that the last to drink would be dead. And soon they were right all along! ...

➤ Enter dogma, the never ending story of past events untold ... The stories to be written are once shy but twice bitten ... The olden days of yore to be into the walls of the few past courage to be spun into the village of the few told to be the torrid facts of the pinnacle stories ... The foes of the plenty few that in this day, be that of the fallen ... To be into the night of blinding light that speaks of itself in high order, but without order to be told to be into the beam, the one that is ever constant ... Or as constant as it were to seem...

➤ There we see the meeting being held in the ball room of sorts ... The meeting room, as it is called by the one so proclaimed as High Order ... The head of the estate has called this meeting of Saturday, morning ... Conscious and Unconscious have equal share, though Conscious has higher order during times of awakenings ... As the daily occurrences are being dealt out, and taken care of by each head of state, as it were to be called ... Spleen arrives at work, says hello to his secretary, places his hat on the rack and coat alike, and enters his office as such; and proceeds to his window desk ... He overlooks the inbox filled with air and opens the third drawer from the top to revile his six-shooter he keeps; for such occasions as everyday life ... Upon relinquishing the weapon from the drawer prison he keeps it in ... Loaded ... Has it but only one bullet ... What he keeps in his bullet carriage, for again, such occasions as everyday life ... Spin-spin does the clip go, where will it stop, soon he shall know ... To his head he holds it, fast to the trigger his finger is there ... On the count of three he often would dare ... One is then reported, two is next in line ... Three is close behind two, but never once defined ... Alas, he reconciles and puts away his gun ... Better left for another day to plight its personal fun ... As a good day's work has rounded last its call, Spleen heads home again ... Lonely after all...

> If a tree falls in a wood, and no one is around to hear it, does it make a sound? ... Ideally that's a very accurate question ... Of course it does one might say ... I mean, if you were there you would hear it ... So what's to stop it from making said sound even if you weren't there? ... But then, one might have to ponder, what if the tree was asleep when it fell, what then? ... Surely it would fall without a peep, or if it were awake but rather adventurous and enjoyed the danger ... Then there is the opposite end of the spectrum with the types of trees that are loud, proud, or otherwise make lots of noise ... Perhaps one is a screamer ... But then ... Again ... What if said tree were mute, and therefore incapable of making any sound? ... Then there is the aspect of what if you were in Paris? ... *[The city]* ... And you were conversing with a friend over the distinction between the Bagel and the Danish *[Country or food, it's your discussion]*? You believe that the bagel is tender, sweet, and caring, while also delicious and nutritious. Your friend believes that the Danish are an industrious, hard-working group that put out a sound product. You look at your friend quite strange, but you state that the Danish's are also tasty and can be quite nutritious too. Your friend looks back at you quite queasy at your comment, and states that the Danish are a people, not a food. You retort to say that it is breakfast time, and you're hungry; when all of a sudden Superman drops from the sky, looks you dead in the eyes, and recants how he just heard the tiny screams of both a North Wisconsin Cypress, and a red squirrel, as their destinies were about to collide ... Only a split second later, as if he were going into hyperspace, Superman's figure is stretched to bands of color and a crack of a whip is heard

as he instantaneously disappears from sight. *[Flash to the tree fall location]*, Superman appears just as instantaneously between the tree and squirrel, merely inches from uncertain doom for either party ... Placing the tree on the ground, out of harm's way, Superman then sits at the squirrel's tea party table and insists on having a crumpet. To which he is denied due to the squirrel having finished off the last one in a haste to gorge and satisfy his last moments here, before being nothing more than a flat, hairy tree-kill diskette ... With his heart hung low, having his hopes dashed, Superman returns to the air, hungry and alas, lonely again ... He returns to his fortress on the moon...

➤ The Writings On The Wall

o   If you knock on wood today, be careful of the way, you look at, the writings on the wall...

o   Do you see them; can you hear them, creep up behind you? Down they look upon you head and write a thing or two. Under the skin is deep within the captivating smile. The jester stands a while, waiting on the king...

o   Poetry in motion; sickens like the ocean, while standing in the bottom of the boat. Hold on very tightly; and stand there mostly slightly, until it's time to leave. When it's time to pack and go, do it fast and watch the flow. When you arrive at your final destination, tell me how it was. Did you enjoy the ride along the fuzz? ...

o   I write it down so I can remember; otherwise the ideas are lost forever. Never to be repainted on the scene. Most I write is of dark matter, or a trail along a path unknown. To which there is but no one home...

o   In the middle of the night I can hear the kite, calling me to play my plight. And I say to thee, "Neigh, nary will I go into the night and fill the sky with thyne plight, to which there is no end in sight!" "You must be mistaken," said thee, "It is but the wind that beckons me!" Again I worry for your soul, and again you beg me for control. I slash at you with my butter knife, as you strife toward me with ill content. And suddenly you attract me without a sense of unrelent! At the end of the night whence dawn hath shown; the sense of carnage with a hint of bone; again we meet and say our best to describe last night's unrest. But tomorrow will again be told. The only thing to do is just be bold. And that my friends, is truth be told! ...

     o   A bit of inspiration for the nation, an erection feels like pure perfection, makes one want to commit an election without any sense of direction but up! ...

     o   Think about all that's read, burn these images inside one's head. Because one day you will be dead, if nothing more than blood spread. Take with you this truth I dread, the world is against your home and bed; kill the politics to control the writings on the wall as short ... Life isn't a game, it's a sport! One not for spectators, I must retort! ...

    ➢ I will leave you be. Pressing business at hand, the monkeys have teamed up with the penguins and have posed a front on the entrance to my bathroom! I cannot even take a shit without them watching me! Those beady little eyes, so cute yet so evil! ...

\\FIN//

About The Author

W. M. Sharp has spent most of his life doing this job, or the next. He grew up in a little town, on an island in the middle of the Pacific Ocean. It was such a nice and peaceful life. He joined the military at a young age and traveled around. Upon exiting the service, he decided to attend college; he graduated with an AS in Pre-Medicine, and is pursuing a BS in Psychology, while also writing.